West Richardson Street

Street

A novel about High Wycombe

By Saqib Deshmukh

Saqib Deshmukh

First published in 2014 by INDUS VALLEY FUNK PRODUCTIONS

Broken Content: writings of Saqib Deshmukh

http://saqib67.wordpress.com/

ISBN-13: 978-1494976651

To Iqbal

Dig deep !

Sajid

August 9th 2015

In memory of Christina Maritos, Shaukat Amin and Nadeem Javed
and all those that we have lost along the way.

Dedicated to those that need to know and all the lost souls....

Thanks & acknowledgements:

Anjli

Amar & Aisha – my kids for not making too much fuss whilst I was 'away'

My folks

Lennox Carty and Pravin Patel for continuing to believe in me

Firzana, Saika & rest of Green St Crew

Em Hussain

Zia Ullah (for being a brother in arms and fellow traveler on these roads)

Shahid Ahmed

Jaydev Mistry

Leonie Kapadia

To all the young guns coming through

Foreword

Walking down the road
What do you see?
A whole heap of people living a reality
At times you feel you're in the story tuning into a mix of English and Punjabi.
Saqib has captured a community in its struggle
Watching young people caught up in the hustle,
And the fascist and the skinheads looking for trouble.
It gives you a snap shot of the tensions between Asian, African Caribbean and Europeans,
Bringing together individuals, groups and gangs in a struggle for position and power.
Which ignited the fuse causing an explosion of corruption, drugs and prostitution that still affects the town today a political hot potato that's still growing
Down West Richardson Street.
How many roads have you walked down and seen the replica of West Richardson Street
How many times have you been standing watching doing nothing?
How many times have you been seen running?
With tear gas canisters exploding around your feet
How many times have you been walking down a street?
Can you count the racist people you meet?
How many times have you been walking down the street?
And the silence was broken by a screaming mob
Chanting better pay, better job then to be told.... *Shut your gob!*
How many times have you been walking down a street?
Were you brave? Were you coming from a rave?
Were you acting weird? Were you scared?
What sounds can be heard, were you walking with your bird?
Did you walk in a turd?
How many times you been walking down a street
And you feeling the heat of the bobby on the beat?
How dem block off the street
And you exit discrete not a soul did see it.
The things you want to do.... you can't complete
All because you get caught up in what was happening on the street.

Lennox Carty, Dub poet/writer April 2014

Timeline

4000BC-42AD	Hill Fort/Iron age fort at Desborough Castle
150-170AD	Roman Villa built on Rye (abandoned in 4th century) and possible site for main holy well in Wycombe by Holywell Mead.
799	First mention of 'Wichama' - Wycombe
1230	First mention of the ancient road 'Strata de Dusteburg' which ran where Desborough Road/Green St School lies now and linked to the Icknield Way
1239	First Jewish person recorded living in Wycombe
1180-1239	Hospital of St. John created
1642	Battle of Wycombe during Civil War
1665-66	Black plague hits Wycombe - 96 deaths recorded
1828	Goodearl Deeds state refer to an ancient way that led across the open meadows that was most likely linked to Desborough Road.
1830-31	Paper mill 'swing' riots
1849	Board of Health report on Newlands health conditions in Wycombe.
1883	Skeletons found whilst widening Water Lane (later Desborough Road) possible location of medieval leper hospital.
1901	**Annie Shaw** born in High Wycombe
1914	Strike disturbances involving 1500 to 2000 individuals in High Wycombe put down by Police using truncheons. Damage to factories
1932	Desborough Road School destroyed in fire

1935	**The Assassin** born in West Wycombe
1937	**Patricia Shaw** born in Saunderton
1947	Mrs Emily Maud 'Woman housebreaker' of Baker St arrested after 28 cases over two years. She is given three years in prison.
1960	Complaints raised about numbers of 'coloured' immigrants in Furniture industry in the town. **Sally Shaw** born in Bledlow Ridge
1962	Mohinder Singh Hothi, **Mandy's** father came to UK from Punjab.
1965	**Asif's** father Mohammed Hussain came from Pakistan to Wycombe
1967	West Indian Edwin Benedict Francis shot dead in Roberts Road High Wycombe.
1968	Asian delegation from Kenya meet the then Wycombe MP John Hall to protest about new immigration Bill and Enoch Powell speaks in High Wycombe on June 21st
1970	Pakistani Kitchen Porter Toochir Ali murdered in Bow, London and Two thousand Pakistani's march to Downing St to protest against racist attacks
1972	Stuart Hall stated that the housing in the town was responsible for 'artificial segregation'
1974	Commons Select Committee on Race Relations visit High Wycombe to look at the state of racial discrimination in industry.
1975	Cannabis in radioactive waste drums smuggled into UK by High Wycombe man
1975	Balder Chahal (a key leader of the Turban Action Committee) arrested in High Wycombe for not wearing a helmet whilst on a motorbike.

1977	**Asif Hussain** born in High Wycombe General.
1978	**Mandeep Kaur Hothi (Mandy)** born in Slough
1980	Akhtar Ali Baig murdered in East Ham
1981	British Nationality Act 1981 passed
1981	Riots in High Wycombe
1983/84	African-Caribbean man murdered in the International Café, Desborough Road
1983	**Shiraz** born in Aylesbury
1987	High Wycombe proclaimed one of the ten wealthiest towns in Britain. **Stacey Shaw** born in Aston Clinton, Buckinghamshire
1988	'Race Riot' in Paul's Row, High Wycombe
1998	Police in High Wycombe apologise to young Asian men for heavy handed Policing in the town Centre
2001	9/11 and Riots in Oldham, Bradford and Burnley
2002	Armed raid on International Café, Desborough Road
2003	Mohammed Kayani begins an 11 year jail sentence for dealing in heroin and cocaine and for preparing and consuming the drugs in the cafe.
2004	Natasha Darby shot dead in Multi-Racial Centre.
2005	Terrorist bombings in London
2005	Beverley James, a local prostitute dies of heroin overdose on West Wycombe Road
2006	Anti-terrorist raids in High Wycombe
2007	**Mandy** murdered in West Richardson Street
2007	Mohammed Mahroof taxi driver murdered in town

'I shall desire and I shall find

The best of my desires;

The autumn road, the mellow wind

That soothes the darkening shires.

And laughter, and inn-fires.'

Rupert Brookes

"I can't pretend to be a lion able to conquer the enemy,

To master myself would be enough.

I am only the dust on my Lover's path

and from dust I will rise and turn into a flower"

Hazret Maulana Rumi

'Life is one big road with a lot of signs, signs and more signs you've got to make up your mind to face reality all the time'

Badmarsh & Shri/Tenor Saw/Bob Marley

Map of Desborough Road area. High Wycombe

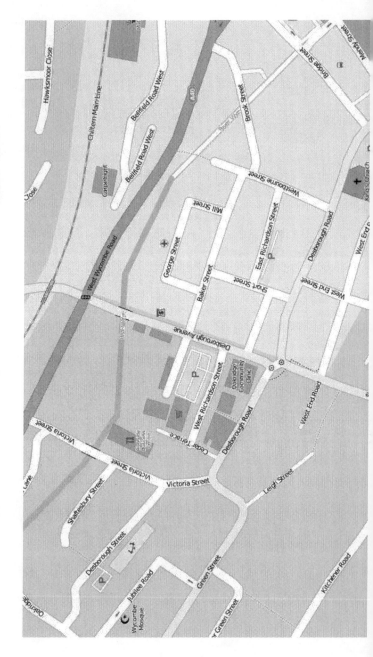

WEST RICHARDSON STREET: FAMILY TREES

SHIRAZ ALI

SHIRAZ ALI

HUSSAIN ALI
FATHER

SHENAZ ALI
MOTHER

ASIF HUSSAIN

ASIF HUSSAIN

MOHAMMED HUSSAIN
FATHER

ATIA HUSSAIN
MOTHER

MANDEEP HOTHI

MANDEEP HOTHI

MOHINDER HOTHI
FATHER

PARMINDER KAUR
MOTHER

OTHER CHARACTERS:

THE ASSASSIN

AKKY

DON

DANNY RAJA

PC SAMINAH KHAN

BASH

MANGY

HIGH WYCOMBE

Prologue: The Road

'Hope cannot be said to exist, nor can it be said not to exist. It is just like roads across the earth. For actually the earth had no roads to begin with, but when many men pass one way, a road is made.'

Lu Xun

He walked on the narrow path of shingle and chalk; the hills surrounded him dark and foreboding promising nothing as he ventured further down the Old Windsor Way. The path grew wider and there were some huts and settlements by a holy well with some old Roman ruins. He crossed a small wooden bridge over the Wye and saw smoke in the distance. He passed some pilgrims dressed in black and a cart trundled by full of wheat on a road that was flooded. Someone said that the path was called St Margaret's and if he kept walking he would find the hospital for lepers but when he got there he found a school and children playing in the light of sunset. The smoke grew darker and he saw some signs 'Wharton and Sons' and chairs standing outside shops. The children came back from the school but now they were dressed in rags and smelt of old potatoes. He turned and walked through puddles of dark water and a woman scrubbing her step. She looked at him and carried on. Soon the skies went dark and he heard trains and coaches and saw children being sent to new houses. He kept walking and the skies eventually cleared and he approached the old Victorian building with a boys and a girls sign outside it. A young black boy skipped past him and went into a shop selling mangos and spices and he heard the call to prayer outside a large terraced house. He knocked on the door and waited.

Chapter One

'Days and months are travelers of eternity. So are the years that pass by. Those who steer a boat across the sea, or drive a horse over the earth till they succumb to the weight of years, spend every minute of their lives travelling. There are a great number of ancients, too, who died on the road. I myself have been tempted by the cloud-moving wind filled with a strong desire to wander.'

Basho

There's all this land in between that people never see. The same land that was lost when the land grabs came and when the roads and railways encroached. The paths had always been there plotted against the landscape taking pilgrims and potatoes and before them the ancients. There were only a few old names left and 'A' roads. The open fields and meadows that had been so abundant had been enclosed and fallen into private hands. The wells and then the mills which had drawn people to the town had all but gone with again only their names being left behind to give people a clue to what had stood before. People now drive and walk down roads with no thought to the previous journeys that had taken individuals down these very same paths. Those who came to work in the mills after being taken off the land after hearing of the money that could be earned throughout the year and not just at harvest time. They came from the regions - Ireland and Wales in particular to make their lives in this valley to join the chair making fraternity and dig the deep embankments needed for the new train lines that were spreading west. They came from St Vincent in the jet stream of the Windrush to become carpenters and joiners and they were soon joined by men from Mirpur and Kashmiris, whose families had been displaced by the Mangla dam. In time all became factory fodder in the furniture industry where labour was needed in jobs, and in times where the white man was not interested. New roads and new houses were built to reflect this expansion and the town grew exponentially where previously there had been unconnected hamlets and villages. A few of the old paths remained but with the push for property and modernity the old ways were quickly forgotten. The pubs and taverns remained for half a century, only for some to ironically become places of worship with a different kind of spirit consumed.

1913

Annie waited in the grounds of the Parish Church. Her fellow hooligans tooled up were waiting for her command so they could wage war against the scabs and black legs. They would marshal the troops from Baker Street, the Westbourne crew and the notorious West End girls who would hide behind the Desborough Arms pub. Her family's anger about their lives as working folk had been transmitted to her. People in the valley were making do and surviving and up the hill and on West Wycombe road there was another world that she could glimpse tantalisingly. The rooms where the furniture her family made ended up. To her those scabs were about destroying her world and her entering that one as a servant. She wanted revenge on these roads.

Annie and her crew were legendary. Her small band of Wycombe's finest social misfits had in the space of a few short months in 1913 caused havoc and mayhem. They attacked strike breakers and the families of the scabs particularly those children who clearly had money during these 'merciless times' as her Dad put it. These shameless harlots would walk around with sweets bulging in their pockets and the latest comics taunting the children of strikers and flaunting their wealth. Annie and her merry men (she was the only girl) would liberate these gentlemen and women of their belongings and make sure they were redistributed to the towns poorest in Newlands. This, of course, brought her into conflict with the town's constabulary who hated her and her father with extraordinary passion but also with fear at what they could unleash.

1963

Mohammed Hussain had missed the train. He was due to go to a place called Sheffield where his cousin was staying. He clutched a small notebook with some choice words in English in case he had got lost. Ali *bhai jaan* had insisted that he take it with him when he left London. October 1963 was cold and damp and he saw this in the faces of the *angrez* that he met - ruddy red complexions and the smells of woodbines was all the impression that he had of them. The stares he could deal with - he remembered how the British were stared at when they came to his village Jada and when the men came with suits to start the work on the dam. Mohammed had met a brother at the station who was going to High Wycombe which was closer to London than Sheffield and decided to risk it. He had heard from his cousin in Luton that they had started to take on Asians in the furniture factory and he had always been good with his hands.

1981

Shenaz Ali was sick and tired of being a translator for her Pakistani kindred. As soon as a few village women found out that she could read and write English they were at her door with their crazy mountain talk. She was lucky that she had picked some up and together with her rudimentary Punjabi she was able to converse and give support. Many of them didn't even consider themselves to be Pakistani but instead talked about being Kashmiri, which she found odd as the country didn't exist and half of it was occupied by India. She had looked forward to coming to England and living with family in London but she found herself living down a road which was slowly becoming little Mirpur. There were one or two Lahori families but Urdu speakers like her were in a minority and lived over the other side of town in a place called Totteridge which was much hillier if not the mountainous place that she imagined from the name. She had been told about the fine Grammar schools in the area and her husband had assured her that they would be moving to a bigger house once they started a family:

"I don't want to hear your *nukray larkee.* There are Pakistani men who are still living two, three to a room in this town. When they make me a manager at the Post Office we'll move to Bowerdean I promise"

Her husband was a good man but she did not share his optimism and hope. At home they had servants and helpers and now here in this chair making town she was cooking and cleaning every day and reading trashy Urdu novels. One day she would get a car and get a job; that's what these women needed to see - so many of the new ones completely reliant on their husbands and lacking independence. She had not gone to the most prestigious women's colleges in Karachi to become a mere housewife in this country.

2007

'In this country in 15 or 20 years' time the black man will have the whip hand over the white man'

Enoch Powell, April 1968

He had waited for too long - seen Rome burn and the banks of the river Tiber burst. The time had come for action. Time was ripe and the enemy too confused and disorientated. The information from the other cells had come through and he would be working clean and alone. The signal was clear and at all times it needed to be seen that they were loners, unattached. No one must ever know about the Movement.

He had been delivering babies in Bucks since 1969. Over the years many things had changed. He had got promoted, become a senior member of staff, his own children had got married and divorced, had kids, run away to India or come out as proud gay men during the stormy eighties. He had managed this entirely with the help of his wife. He did not mind progress -what had really stuck in his throat was the number of brown and black babies they had started to deliver in the towns. From the odd one or two every month the wards were now a cascade of coloured faces with the miscegenation phenomena of beige babies where one of the partners was black. He hated this most of all - sometimes it seemed like the white race was declining and the grinning piccaninnies as Powell had put it, were taking over. Soon whole roads that had been a pleasant mix of Joneses and Smiths became a mix of Khans and Hussains with their Caribbean brethren living side by side. He had gone to the park to see a multitude of brown faces wearing whites playing cricket with only a handful of white youngsters in sight. On Market day in the town he could hear hearty St Vincent accents mixed with Panjabi and Hindustani and he knew deep down that this was the way to ruin. That's why he joined up as soon as heard about the organisation and was offered an opening. He had wanted to make a difference for Queen and Country. He wanted to serve and when it became too difficult implementing population control from maternity wards he moved up and out. Infant mortality rates were poor amongst sub-continent babies – something to do with low birth rates and the peculiar custom that some Pakistanis had of marrying their cousins. I suppose he just helped this along. The poor creatures were always upset but would be up the spout in next to no time determined to increase the numbers of their vile race. In many ways he did them a favour as some of these poor women would have died in child birth without his intervention. An adult corpse was always much harder to explain then a pre-born dying in a woman's womb.

2007

Asif counted the wad of twenties in his pocket. The sound of crisp notes pleased him. He'd done well today and the extra pickups paid well. Asif was known for not asking questions - doing jobs that others would turn down. Some of the stuff was on the edge of illegal and some of it was kind of mad. Like transporting groups of women to a Refuge, while trying to avoid their psychotic Pakistani husbands. He was lucky he still had all his teeth. Asif made many journeys in his weekly travels chauffeuring the great and the good to different parts of Buckinghamshire. In between these bigger jobs he would do taxis locally and in his head would retrace some of the former journeys that he made when he was a kid in the town. Going to school, the mosque, his many cousins and then the various places he and his crew would have chilled in. Of course many things had changed - for a start there were more ethnics around. Growing up in the town in the late 80s there was a still a sense that the Asian and Caribbean communities were small and easily located in the town. You knew where you needed to go to get *haldi* and get a fade from the Asian and Caribbean barber shops but now people were everywhere, living in places where he would have not dared walk through let alone reside. You could now get jerk chicken from Asda and once a year all the supermarkets would do Ramadan offers.

For Shiraz it had almost finished before it began. It was the endless form filling and applications that had almost put him off becoming a Police Community Support Officer. But the worst part was finding out that his parents had made a mistake spelling his name. 'Sheeraz' had become 'Shiraz' on his birth certificate and he subsequently spent 24 years not knowing that the spelling of his name was exactly the same as a bottle of French wine. He decided against changing it as he figured that could be an interesting angle when he talked to fellow women recruits. Shiraz was a predictable young Pakistani middle class man with predictable tastes. But he wanted to stand out and besides the only other Sheeraz he knew was a bit of a prick and he wanted to ensure that there was no confusion in the town. Though not much of a drinker it would give him a certain panache chatting up girls in the pubs and bars that he was hoping to frequent through his newly found career.

Mandy looked at the various men that were passing by the cafe. There was the normal mix of low life, bearded boys and elders who would either avert their vision or look down when they saw her or leer at her lasciviously. One old man had a face like a car park; full of marks and potholes, a product of years of acne, hard work and worry no doubt. He would just stare at her kindly, as if she was in need. Mandy thought he could have been someone who knew her Dad back on the days when she had so many Pakistani and Kashmiri Uncles who would visit the house with their *ladoos* and their pipe smoke. Before the days that they gave up using Bics to shave, they would even have the odd whisky - purely for medicinal purposes of course, they would joke; making out that her Dad was a *Hakeem* and had been sent down by god to be their physician. Once these men rediscovered their faith, the walls went up and her Uncles were no more.

Chapter Two

'Too low to find my way... too high to wonder why...'

Lebanese Blonde, Thievery Corporation

It had been a tough first day for Shiraz. It was bad enough that his fellow trainees had got easier breaks and landed in places where they got an easy ride. It was just his luck that on his first day he had found a body...

When they first found out he was applying for the post people tried to talk him out of it. Told him straight that he would lose respect and no one would talk to him anymore and that being a Police Community Support Officer would give him no end of grief. Maybe they were right he thought when he found her strung out in the skip in the car park.

"*Bheta* have you thought this through?"

He could still hear his *Abbo* questioning his sanity. Shiraz pointed out that his Dad's Uncle had been a copper back home.

"That was in Pindi you stoopid boy - things were different. He was little more than a jumped up *Chowkidaar*"

He'd seen the ad in Asda. In between picking up some *gobi* for his mum he had been checking the fine sister on the Deli counter. Then he saw a group of street urchins congregating by a notice board. Shiraz called them street urchins mainly 'cos of their prickly dispositions but also 'cos they were little pricks. The kind who would set fire to your *Chacha's* shed or scratch up your motor over small change or if you didn't put your head down when you walked past them.

He watched them struggling to read the poster and then intervened. 'Police Community Support Officers wanted' he read out.

"Whats one of them *yaara*? They're payin' 18Gs"

"Who'd wanna work for da *Marvay?*"

"You could do that Sheeru. You're too fuckin' sensible for your own good."

'Me in the cops?' For a second he saw himself in uniform chatting to the *larkee* on the Deli counter and it all seemed to fall into place. He made a note of the number on his mobile and watched the urchins driving off with the shopping trolleys chased by security. Maybe he would try his luck with the girl in the shop. He knew it would be tough and there would be all the normal complications but he was sure that it would give him assistance in his struggles to get laid. It was the same old story - boys were footloose & free & girls were under lock and key. Shiraz struggled with his freedom sometimes and the unfreedoms of the girls he knew. Not even a clean driving license was a route out as brothers invariably controlled the motors. It wasn't anything too profound or deep just centuries of sexism that he was just about able to contemplate & grasp let alone do anything about. But there were women who bugged him in the community - the hijab wearing bitches that stuck their noses up at him, their Dolce Gabbana bags swinging heavy with their accessories and able to cause much damage if needed. They would proclaim their independence in the face of all this; proclaiming their rights, whilst never lifting a finger to challenge any wrongs. They were the worst kind of sisters.

Mandy was screwed – she was down to her last few quid and she was getting desperate for what the *paisa* could get her. Another fix, another night obliterated in the Wycombe fog. Akky and Don provided the key for her lock, to get her the *maal* that would break the pain. She would have to do some tricks tonight, get her on her knees or something and take some man's dick. It made her retch sometimes and the gravel left nasty cuts that she would have to put Dettol on. Where were they? Even Asif was out of town doing some pick up in London. She would end up in a car tonight - in the back seat trying to keep warm. She pulled herself up and looked at the cracked mirror. Touched her hair off her face and laid the foundation on thick. It was going to be another cold night.

She had lived down the road for three years. In fact she had lived 'on road', roughed it in cars and spent one memorable night in the ladies toilets. Most of the time she was in Akky's den with some of the girls. Everyone knew about this place and they just tolerated its existence. Infamously two Pakistani Councillors had been caught with their pants down during a routine drugs raid. She had remembered the money in the envelopes that had been given to all the witnesses in exchange for their silence. The bullshit fabricated story that had done the rounds at the behest of one of the local tribal leaders (who also happened to be the local Labour Party Whip) made out these two jokers were in on the raid and were Police observers. Like many others before them the stain on their characters was 'persilled' away.

Mandeep often tried to guess what lay behind the closed doors of her punters and the great and the good and not so good. Whether it was the *kalmah* or a brass door knob, whether the door opened out to the road or a small front garden or if there was an elaborate gate leading to a path and then a stately double door; there was always a certain amount of intrigue about what happened behind closed doors. Would there be a young 14 year old girl strung out on opiates doing tricks with taxi drivers and lowly local civil servants? A middle class family meal being torn apart as the youngest son declares that he is having a sex change? Or maybe a single parent Kashmiri woman trying to get her only son through the 11+? The permutations were always fairly thrilling and kept her occupied in the downtime that invariably afflicted her. Some people would leave their front doors and whatever happened they would leave everything behind once the door closed. Others; the Blacks, Asians and women and the elderly would wear their problems like a uniform; pain, longing and frustration etched upon worn out faces. Their faces betrayed them constantly and it was hard in her encounters not to be affected.

Asif had seen her again and she had winked at him. Man what was up with him? Thirty two years of age with piccanie and he was still chasing gal. Instead of going home after shifts he'd cruise around as if touting but he'd be looking for her. They called her Mandy but Asif knew her when she just plain Mandeep, the quiet Sikh girl in his class who no one ever messed with 'cos her old man was a wrestler. Not just any wrestler mind, but Junior West Punjab champion 1960. He lost touch with her after leaving school and when her Dad got killed in a hit and run he had gone round the house but she'd left home and run off with a dealer and he left it at that and did not pursue it – he had enough on his plate just being himself. Asif had known for a long time that he was never going to amount to much. Generation of no parents working, a disabled brother and state handouts had slowed down any development he could have had. This with the tendency to fuck up any real opportunities that came his way rendered him fairly useless. Not that driving a taxi was a waste of time - it was just that there were far stupider brothers who were doing this with fewer qualifications than the one GCSE and attendance certificate that he owned. Even the School leaving ceremony had been a farce - boys turning up in a tuxedo and hired limos to collect an empty record of achievement. One of the youth workers who'd been there joked with him that he couldn't believe how much effort these guys had put into it and the importance they placed in getting suited and booted.

"How can you leave somewhere you never went to anyway?"

Least he'd got a couple of certificates but 10 years of school had left him adrift and directionless. Though he made his living from driving he was never a driven man, in a manner of speaking you could say he lacked drive. What had moved him, motivated him in any kind of meaningful wayhad died when he was very young. It had been kicked out of him, extracted from him every time he had opened his mouth in school and then again when he had said nothing in the mosque. A bright inquisitive child, in a few years condemned as factory fodder at best, years later transporting junkies from one part of town to another. The shadows of his former teachers always behind him.

Stacey decided that the jeep had to go. The memories of old boyfriends were bad enough and the sight of Josh pissing on one of the tyres at the Marlow Regatta was still etched in her head. No it just wasn't fitting in to her image as a local credible journalist. She needed to get something more down at heel and downgrade her motor. The poor little rich girl jibes were getting to her and she needed to get rid to get real. Wycombe was full of sperm stained stories and she was too conspicuous in her Suzuki. She'd made her name from last summer events. It wasn't everyday that real live terrorists came to town. Stacey had gone from interviews with blue rinse grannies to Met cops on Gold Command in a matter of weeks.

Her long legs had worked wonders with local young Pakistani men who once smitten gave her the full lowdown. She looked up and down the car and had to admit it wasn't much of a looker. The Honda Civic wouldn't attract much attention and she had to be low key. The whole Home Counties thing was getting her down and even though she could lose the accent and get guttural her breeding always showed through. She knew she was a good writer, and she had a nose for a story. The motor would have to do.

The Surveillance

Modus operandi – meaning method of operation (Latin)

You had to catch the enemy off guard, that's what the manuals said and him and his group would operate in covert ways to carry out it's mission. But the beauty was in the details - there was no sloppy army stuff. He would be up at night meticulously planning operations and building in irrational behaviour and 'what if' scenarios.

The depth of the deception was immense and only a few even within the Movement were aware of some of the activities that were taking place. Rarely there would be mistakes and these would be rectified or blamed upon others. This could be a dodgy death in custody, or a black prisoner falling to his death down a prison landing. But as long as there was paperwork that could be tampered with - autopsies and Coroners reports that could be amended. There were good people in these organisations; his people, that could be influenced relatively easily. They could be persuaded and results created which would leave no trail of detritus for some annoying journalist to chase after. Even they could be disposed of if needed. Each time taking care to be precise and efficient. After all to kill, to remove was easy, but to do so without leaving clues or without any hint of suspicion required class. An attribute he and his colleagues had an abundance of.

Chapter Three

'If light is in your heart, then you will find your way home.'

Rumi

Shiraz had found her in a skip; Asian female, mid to late twenties. He'd seen two Pakistani schoolgirls acting suspiciously locally. Nothing in particular but he knew the routine from training exercises and his own street sense that some of these schoolgirls were not so innocent. Shiraz had polished off the remains of his mum's *Aloo ghobi* from last night and his fellow PCSO Ashley had gone off on her lunch. So it was him mooching round the back end of West Richardson Street. He wasn't sure what made him look. Back in the day he would have scavenged parts to build a go kart or found some dodgy CRT monitor to plug in his brothers LAN rig. Those multi-player Doom games had been crazy. But finding a body, a dead body, his first dead body on his first day on patrol was not something he had planned for. Nothing could have prepared him for what he saw.

'Somebody gonna get hurt real bad.'

The Asian comic's words were ringing in his head. He'd had enough - he had gone through all the interviews and briefings and debriefs. She had died from an overdose and her body dumped in the skip. Don't know if someone panicked after one of the toe rag dealers cut her some dirty gear but they had a body of a 29 year old Asian girl in a mortuary waiting for a coroner's report. Meanwhile the local community closed in on itself and sharpened their knives. There were a few half baked apologies from the great and the good but that was it. The Mosque sent a letter to the Gurdwara while slagging off Sikhs at *jummah* prayers. Some local *goray* just saw this as a continuation of the decline of the area since 'the Asians came'. This shit was not gonna go away he thought it would run and run, the lowlifes would continue to operate with impunity and communities would eventually dismiss it as *kismet.* He knew another girl would appear on the scene and the cycle of supply and demand would continue. His two sisters, who had married into the professional classes never wasted an opportunity to slag these kind of girls off. The assumption being that the majority of young Asian, Pakistani girls were still virgins at the age of 18 and even Shiraz knew that wasn't true.

Asif wasn't mean to her, in fact once sexual intercourse as a formality had been over and done with they had as good a relationship as to be expected between a taxi driver and a working girl. Mandeep did not expect anything from this life so if anything out of the norm was happening which could possibly be construed as being positive she would take it. This could mean cast off clothes and perfumes from his bitchy sisters or a late night dash to Southall to get some *khaana* and hit a sheesha joint. The *kutta* could be good to her even though he would sometimes revert to type when he was with his salivating mates.

She had taken the beatings - she had given some out. Mandy used to laugh at that. They would give her a good kicking - never on the face always had the body, especially if business been slow, she'd pissed off a punter or mainly 'cos they liked beating up women. Then she'd get a guy who would ask her to insert the tip of her heel up his arsehole or those who would ask her to punch them as they were ejaculating. One way or another guys were fucked up. Only Asif broke this mould, gave her some peace/*shanti* during her free time. A little ray of light in the Desborough darkness.

She would often stare into the heart of puddles, at her reflection and the reflections of the environment around her. Sometimes she could detect the paving or the road at the bottom of the puddle, at others time it was too murky and dark, collecting the dirt of the town. However there would be occasions where the water was opaque and what lay underneath would emerge. She would imagine other faces, other times and the lives of others who had lived before her. This town had always had mills & furniture factories and it was these factories that had lured men (and the occasional woman) from the Punjab, Mirpur and St Vincent. This was all according to her long deceased old man but she had no reason to disbelieve him. Truth was that it was written on the faces of the brown and black elders in the town. Bearded devout Pakistani men who had in a previous life chased skirt and had pitched battles with skinheads and the old Caribbean Aunties (she had always called them that from a young age) with their shopping bags and incessant chatter who in their younger days would have been clearing the dance floor at blues parties and taking the Council to court for expelling their sons from school. Her father for all his faults had given her an understanding of community matters and the history of the town from when the 'darkies' came. Some of the stories had not been pretty but made her see the reality of migration to this country and the trials and tribulations built in to these journeys. Her deep thoughts staring into puddles, trying to detect the old cobbled stones underneath would be interrupted by the odd passer-by, but most commonly by local winos and junkies that this part of town attracted. She looked out as the sun began to set behind Tom Burt's Hill.

It was a dark night, proper dark as there were a whole lot of broken street lights down this street. No one ever complained - the cover of darkness could cover up many things. But the path beyond led to the woods and the pitch black. Now that was a place you did not want to find yourself on your own - a single brown female with a fake Gucci handbag. Even though you could hear the traffic in the distance no one could hear you and that was the problem. Sometimes Mandeep dragged Asif up here in the summer and they'd go for a walk and pretend they were in the countryside and maybe a proper couple but sooner or later woodland would meet suburban roads and reality. She looked up at the cold moon with its ring of clouds and wondered how it might have been before the street lights and how girls like her would have existed. Imagining Wycombe was more obtainable than Jalandhar and her Punjabi heritage was mainly a distant memory, particularly on a night like this. She used her lighter to guide the way and walked up the path. There was a bench further up and she fancied being a recluse right now. It was only a few minutes in and if she screamed someone surely would notice. Back then they would have lit a fire in these woods and there would have been fire places in the little terraces she was leaving behind. Instinctively she picked up some dry grass and twigs - she knew what she was going to do, even though she had not done it before. The small fire was blazing now and she was proud of herself for getting it started. The flames illuminated the trees around her and crackled as she burnt the dry wood and grass. She did not notice the man that had been drawn to the light, and as he crept into her frame of vision she was startled. He was a middle aged Pakistani guy who stared at her. He reached out and gave her some yellowing newspaper that she accepted and put on the fire in long strips.

Stacey could feel that the story was coming together piece by piece. Vice, murder and the Asian community in the centre of Wycombe.

She could just smell the story and her journalist instincts were kicking in big style. Stacey knew that she was only a few front pages away from the Nationals and she could kiss this shitty little town goodbye.

However she was getting sick of getting close to her Asian contacts on the ground. What was it with these guys and garlic? They must have thought she was born yesterday with the kind of rubbish they were throwing at her. She knew about the paedo taxi company, the slimy community leaders having business lunches with women in Beaconsfield, even the Councillors who were turning a blind eye to their rented properties being turned into crackhouses. No she wanted the real dirt, the filth and degradation that lay underneath the surface.

"So let's start again - number 62 *Mungater* Avenue has a Hezbollah cell running a curry for guns racket"

"Yea *kusmay*, I mean it's true... My brother's wife, her uncle heard about it from the guy who cuts his hair. You said 50 notes right?"

"I need some proper evidence matey. You got any photos, letters. I can't write a newspaper article based on some dodgy gossip from your Auntie."

"It was my brother's wife's uncle. Proper close family. They got a kebab van on the estate. Give me 20 then"

She took some new notes out from her purse and handed it over to him.

"Next time I want some pukka stuff. Hard facts Akky otherwise I'm going elsewhere"

She wanted to crack this story - she was getting tired of writing about white people in Buckinghamshire going to Africa every week. Even she knew that the days of civilising missions were long gone it was just a shame the more privileged residents of the County had not clocked on to this fact.

Raven's People

Raven's People were born in the late 50's by disillusioned fascists unhappy with the direction of travel of the Nationalists in the country. Everywhere Empire was falling and their Black subjects were descending on the UK in their masses. It was not a pressure group for the likes of Chesterton and Lord Haw Haw to push their ideology of racial preservation but to tackle the problem at its core - the extermination of these subjects in the most clinical and efficient way. Inspired by the ideologue Alexander Raven Thomson the core of this group resided in deepest Buckinghamshire and Berkshire, counties with a strong link to the Crown and the Chiltern's Hundreds and with towns where communities of Asian & West Indian people had now settled. He had offered his services early on and once he received his instructions he knew very early on what he had to do and what was required of him. Since those heady days of the sixties he had taken part in a slow genocide of black and browns in the sleepy towns of the shires. Enoch, the fine patriot came and went but he ridiculed the skinheads and the Blood and

Honour jokers who followed him. No class or breeding there and their inane 'paki bashing' antics had infuriated him as they were neither effective nor subtle.

The Cleansing

There were always ways and means to solve problems and deal with barriers to any mission. Always ways to subvert and divert attention. He had got into the room in between the baboon at the front going for a very long toilet break. This break normally involved consuming a considerable amount of white powder up his nose. He had needed to check that the process that he had initiated had been successful. The contact in Amersham had been most useful and handed over significant amounts of police data. He drew comfort from facts, from names and addresses as it unraveled a chain, a chain of information that had led him to this road and to this flat. Over a period of time he had observed the workings of this particular food chain and unravelled the main players - the victims and the prey. The rest, well the rest fell into place. There was some contamination, disturbing the delicate eco-system that was in place. He prided himself on carrying out a discreet operation with no flourishes and signatures to his name. By interjecting, by placing certain materials into the process he and his colleagues had learnt how the impact of their actions spiraled and their work was done by others through a chain reaction. They fed into the revenge culture that was the heart of these communities.

It was not a conspiracy; it was in the public interest. It worked like this:

Step one:

You ensured that the supply of drugs to a inner city local with a sizable black or brown population was not blocked or interrupted in any way. Of course there would be raids and Operations, arrests would be made and then under the guise of developing an informant culture people were released. It was a game of containment, a way of gathering information but most of all it created a space for them to intervene.

Step two:

You staged an intervention - this could be in all manner of ways - contaminating the drug supply, cutting it with Vim or rat poison and releasing it. You would set up a situation where two warring factions were at each other's throats by giving a beating to one of their inner circle. There were many other techniques honed over the decades all designed to wreak havoc.

Step three:

His personal favorite was stepping back to watch the fireworks. This would lead to a number of fatalities and would assist in the organisations objectives. Sparks would fly and these men so enraged and consumed by their localized anger would assassinate each other in glorified gangland killings. The local press would have a field day but nobody would be upset or raise their concerns about the body count as 'they would have it coming to them'.

He did not like to describe his operations as vermin control - that was the language his counterparts used. He was performing a civic function that in another guise he would be championed as a captain of industry. However he found that this was much more fun and the job satisfaction much more rewarding. When he found her in the early hours of the morning she was already dead, the current heroin supply had been cut with rat poison in a controlled way, all that was left was for him to use the baboon's car to dispose of the body. With the gloves on he slipped out of the ground floor flat and with a glance both ways opened the Honda Civic parked outside. He drove slowly into West Richardson Street and dumped her in the skip leaving the car back where he found it. With the gloves removed he went back to his Volvo and took out a handkerchief and his glasses case. He mopped his brow put his glasses on and drove off.

Asif stared down the hill. He'd always been attracted to the copse, a circle of trees in Castlefield. Locals called it Desborough castle but they'd never been a castle there just some weird mound. Some days he'd drive up, get out of the car and light a cig up. Today he'd walked up there 'cos it was sunny and it made sense. He'd unravel his thoughts and try and make sense of it all. It was peaceful up here, sure you could still hear the traffic but there'd be birds as well. He knew the countryside was all around him but it was nice that he had a piece of it on his doorstep. He spent most of his life on the roads of this town, as a kid running down back alleys and paths all over Desborough, Sands and Castlefield. He'd played footie on the roads and on a few occasions had only missed being hit by Datsuns and Ford Cortinas that were all the rage at the time. But he had been spared the worst - some mans were still on road - shotting, selling stolen gear and running around on missions. Spent so much time living on road that they were almost part of them as much as the dodgy pot holes and blind spots you needed to keep an eye on when you drove through the town. At least he had family around him and could make a living that did not involve suspect packages. Selling *maal* was such a big part of the local economy and had put *roti* (as well as the keys to some fine 4x4s) on the tables of some quite well established families in the area. These lads and their female counterparts were on road and nothing would move them from this station in life.

He'd heard about the body and when he found out who it was he sobbed for six hours. He hadn't even cried that much when his wife had miscarried the first time. Mandy had been his world and the few hours a week that he spent with her gave his life a risky dimension that he craved. Asif drove around looking for her face for days and then when it dawned on him that he would never see her again he went into revenge mode looking for her killer. He only stopped when the Police called him in as a possible suspect:

"We have evidence to show that Mandeep Hothi was known to you"

"Yes"

"Did you have a sexual relationship with this woman?"

"Yes I did"

"Were you a punter who went to her premises?"

"Yes but she was also my customer - she would use my cab"

They released him without charge. Heartbroken.

Chapter Four

'When there's no more room in hell, the dead will walk the earth.'

George A. Romero, Dawn of the Dead

Shiraz was getting nowhere chasing leads and only the *haldi* taste in his mouth was getting him through the day. It reminded him of his *Ammi* and yea he had no problem admitting he was a Mummy's boy. But none of this was helping him today. No one was talking and the local sex trade was quiet - they must be shagging their wives instead he thought. It was only the usual suspects and himself who were actually bothered. An Asian young woman had been murdered literally on people's doorstep and there was your usual wall of silence and even Pakistani officers and local Community workers were finding the door well and truly shut. One of the few elders who he had spoken to had called it a 'blood-letting'. The death of a girl was almost the price that had to be paid:

"As long as it's not my daughter"

Even the *shaytaan* couldn't have done this - the girl's body was praying on his mind. He wasn't devout or a born again but he would take his old man to *jummah* prayers now and again and Eid was always big in his house. Shiraz would joke with his mates that he was a bad Muslim 'cos he didn't drink much but no one got his twisted sense of humour. What he wasn't was two-faced, and this was a town full of peeps with multi-faceted personalities.

Asif spent as much time as he could with Mandy. The rollup conversations that he had with her were always the best:

"What so she never suspects a ting"

"I dunno Mandy she don't really talk to me"

"You ever try and talk to her?"

"I think it was Christmas 2002 - we both got drunk at a Holiday Inn. I think that's when Riswan happened."

"So you saying that you ain't talked to your Mrs for five years?"

"We talk we just don't communicate"

"So why d'ya talk to me then?"

He smacked her arse and smiled

"Cos you give me what I want."

"No really Asif tell me please"

"Maybe 'cos I ain't married to ya. Stuff don't get back to in-laws and cousins and fuckin' relatives livin' under my bed"

"You got family living under your bed"

"You know what I mean - only place I got to get some privacy is the shed. I like this arrangement with you and me. I get some space"

"So what do I get out of it?"

"I watch yer back Mandy. Make sure lowlife scumbags are careful with you"

He stroked her face and her phone went off followed by his.

"Heathrow"

"Downley"

She kissed him quickly and ran to a passing Audi coupe. The driver nodded to Asif he nodded back and started the car.

The images were blurry at night. The camera would catch them moving in and out of the shadows. Orange coloured lights moving in the darkness and then headlights getting closer then stopping and girls bending over a window. They would talk for a few seconds and then invariably get into the car. No sound on the camera just the image of a girl making a sale. Some of the punters were ok. Some were evil looking bastards who sweated like hippos when they were humping. Some of her customers would even be whispering prayers whilst in coitus. The odd one would treat her rough and grab her hair. She hated those who mounting her would start swearing at her in Punjabi calling her a slut and it would continue as they withdrew. The rest would hardly say two words as they were so overcome by their shame and it took ages to get their pricks hard. It was a shit way to make some corn but she had other things on her mind. She was done with people making the remarks and talking about him and her. As far as she was concerned it was a closed book. The contents of this chapter had been decided a long time ago but too many people wanted to drag it out and rewrite it. Only she and Asif knew the ending and it would hopefully be away from the roads that controlled her life.

The Polish are everywhere Asif thought. Mans were into plumbing and building and everything. Soon they'd start doing taxis and then there would be trouble. Still nobody was saying no to the Polish girls coming on the scene either on the game or in town. Most of the Pakis saw them as fresh meat and continuing the love/hate thing that Asian blokes had with white women. Speaking of which that sexy white journalist had been hanging around again with her long legs and hint of cleavage. Only a few guys now talked to her, some of the saddos and mentally disturbed types in the community. They'd peddle the same line to her whilst cumming in their *chadees*. She would take their words as gospel/*Quran-Sharif* and next thing he knew it would be front page of the local rag. He seemed to be thinking and worrying about stuff more than he used to – maybe it was all part of getting old and remembering the past however difficult that was for him. Retracing his former footsteps was hard when his former schools were no longer there, when buildings had been demolished and when his former friends no longer had a role in his life. He struggled with the latter the most. Some had got religious and though he found it hard himself he was jealous of the clarity of their faith and single-mindedness. His own lifestyle choices were frowned upon but he knew that he too would succumb one day and he would become someone's bearded uncle and curse modern life whilst hiding a very modern past. The ones however he hated the most were the 'professionals' - he was genuinely glad that some people had made it and got out the ghetto but what he couldn't understand was the snobbish and condescending attitudes that this then created. That somehow due to them having a job that didn't involve serving, driving or doing security that they were better than everyone else. Life at the bottom was tough. When you were at the lower rungs of the food chain mans did not want to know you and Asif knew that she knew this. It did not take a nuclear scientist to work out the desperation of their situation and he did not know any boffins in the circles he moved in. That's not to say there weren't brainy people around - there were guys who knew all their fractions and could make calculations on the fly, but they put their intelligence to use at a lower level to make sure they got paid every time and that no one could touch them not even the Feds.

Stacey could tell when the editor was interested or not. What made good and bad copy. His palms would get sweaty and he would look at her lustfully. Stupid dickhead didn't even know he was doing it. Most of the time she could get her own way - a hand through her hair or a touch to his knee - Stacey could play him as easy as a school recorder. Middle aged blokes in middle management got so jittery around young 'feisty' things like her. She'd overheard one of the Features columnists describe her like that and it had always stuck in her head. She would sit in the Sunshine Café on Desborough Road for hours on end working on leads but also working through some of these thoughts. She knew that the taxi drivers would come in for cup of tea. She could then glean the latest gossip from them and all the comings and goings. Her presence and the pretty Polish girl behind the counter would create the perfect environment for her to weave her craft. She would get by on black coffee and custard creams and staring at the people traffic on Desborough Road. She knew the regular patterns of the road and its side streets. She would also get by on her looks and skills at dealing with people. Round the corner they had found the girl's body in a skip. It made sense to be here, to dig; she knew that Mandy had come in here and that some of the locals had been her punters.

Mandy looked out through the windows of the flat. It was raining again and the guttering on the flat roof below was overflowing. It gushed out like the libido of the men in the town. She had never felt sorry for herself - she was too far gone for that, but the relentless demand for sex in the town amazed her. Most of her customers were married; even the ones who tried to hide it were easy to spot. Maybe they weren't getting enough at home maybe what she & others were offering was risk. She could smell them when they entered the room - it was a stale smell of pre-cum & poppadoms, of cheap cigarettes from Lahore & a faint reminder of a perfume that their daughters may have given them. For more religious types this was always Arab non-alcoholic perfume that she grew to hate. Maybe it was meant to cover up all the above mentioned but it smacked of guilt, of putting it on to mask a smell rather than have a shower. Only a few of her clients ever bothered to.

1913

There had been a deception - he did not know how those boys got their guns. He was not sure why they had shot out the windows and why they pointed up to the air and fired when the police officer from the Metropolitan force had shot at them direct. Why no one recognised the boys from the town and that why when they had been captured they were released the next day without charge. What he did know was that the shooting outside Temple Mills was not an accident but preplanned by the factory owners. The next day the Trades Council made an urgent announcement condemning the incident and calling for immediate talks to settle the lock out dispute. Kevin knew as one of the lieutenants of the movement he would be challenging the lily livered leadership of the Trades Council and main unions in place. What he needed to do is make sure that the workers got the best deal and that Annie and his family were looked after if anything was to happen to him. Annie had grown up in the struggle, the rough and tumble of street politics had hardened her and that she also had her Mother's fiery Irish temper meant that she was well known to the local constabulary which was no mean feat for an eleven year old girl in the town. Kevin had been a witness to the event as he came out of a pub on Frogmoor and he knew that there would be many battles ahead on the roads of the town.

Chapter Five

'I met my love by the gas works wall
Dreamed a dream by the old canal
I Kissed my girl by the factory wall
Dirty old town
Dirty old town'

The Pogues/Dubliners 'Dirty Old Town

Shiraz knew the idiot boys he was trying to talk to. He'd gone to college with one of their brothers and he was still recovering from the experience. Shiraz tried to ensure that it did not cloud his judgment but he knew that he would have to question them.

"Is there a reason you've got the scarf under your hoodie almost covering your eyes?"

"Sheru it's cold blud"

"That's PCSO Ali to you Akil"

He didn't know why he wasted time with these lads and then thought about what he was like when he was their age. Shiraz could still remember Rawalpindi, he used to love going back 'home' till he realised they were just humoring him and his real 'home' was in Booker but he loved the freedom of walking from house to house and the doors always being open. He remembered his Uncle slapping him so hard he went deaf for a week and the mad dogs who would gather in packs on the outskirts of the city. Closer to 'home' he remembered the first time a white friend came around his house and the look on his mum's face when she first saw him. A few weeks later she'd be pulling his cheeks & calling him her *chitta gora*. I think it had an impact on him as the last he had heard of Simon/Cimraan (as his mum called him) he was selling timeshare in Goa. He recollected the dumb Paki tutor his family had hired to get him through 11+. They had split the money between them and Shiraz had ended up tutoring him into University. His family had so little faith in boys doing well academically they were prepared to blow their hard eared rupees on some dumb arse from back home that had a fake degree from *Tutta* University. Well with half the boys down his road having 3 GCSE's between them you couldn't blame them.

Asif really couldn't remember too much about his childhood. Maybe he blocked stuff out 'cos most of it involved the back of his dad's hand. Sure there were some good times but mainly it had been hard and he preferred not to dwell on the past. Compared to Mandy's life his had been a bed of *gulabs* - he still had his own hair and had only been cautioned once in his life. So all things considered he was doing Ok, not brilliant but just Ok. Tariq his disabled brother had died in hospital when he was young and he remembered how happy his family had been coming back from the hospital. Asif remembered the time before mobile phones when folks would talk to each other at street corners and from their backyards. His mates lived on a handful of roads around his house and he would see them every day after school anyway. They hardly ever had any use of a phone. Asif had been 15 the first time he had made an outgoing call. As he got older they would congregate around red call boxes as some lucky lad talked to a girl. He marveled at the large phone in his uncle's car and one or two office types with their pagers. Back in the day Asif's communication needs had been minor with his crew all around him.

Mandy would often think about the past at those times where she had time to think. She'd remember the stupid conversations she had with her friends in Primary schools and who they would marry and what they would wear. Mandy knew that she would never get married now. She was too far gone and didn't think anyone would have her either. Asif made her feel good but she knew deep down in her twisted Punjabi world that there was no future in it. She remembered her granddad talk about partition and what the Muslims did to them. It didn't make much sense then, and only as she got older could she piece it together. Her encounters with Muslims in the town made her realise how deep some of the hatred ran.

Tales of Danny Raja

Let's get this straight - Danny Raja was a clown. But he was also the most gifted and intelligent bloke that Asif had ever met. He'd lived around the corner but he was a year or two older so they hadn't met at school. Truth was he was nothing special then – just another *Jhelum* lowlife with a hoodie. He just changed after his sixteenth birthday. Whatever made him Danny Raja and connected him to the neighbourhood went beyond his partaking off magic mushrooms by Roundabout wood or the week long benders he would go on. He was one of the guys who was probably stranger when he was sober and not charged. Some of the things that Danny got up to were legendary and were embedded in the folklore of these roads. Only talking about his demise broke the laughter and the tears. They had been blessed to be around him, and when he took his fall a lot fell with him or fell right into line.

Asif smiled thinking about the time Danny led a one man crusade against all the fast food places in Desborough Road and Green St. The brother had been outside these shops with his placard and leaflets challenging the staff and punters. He would just tell folks that the food was killing them and they needed to eat stuff that was made with love so they in turn would spread love. Danny hated the fact that all these crews were eating out rather than eating their Mum's roti. It got so bad that Super Fish took out a banning order against him which meant that he was not allowed on the pavement outside - he just climbed a balcony by the new shiny shopping centre and shouted abuse at them. Crazy thing was Danny always made sense -

no one could fault the strength of his arguments in English or in Mirpuri. The guy could drop it hard and even the local imams were in awe of him. But unsurprisingly Danny made enemies - shop and taxi base owners, some of the bigger dealers and most of the Asian Councillors. He hated those he felt were self righteous and self appointed, their stooges and *chumchay*. In any other generation he would have been 50% village idiot and 50% shaman. His folks had moved back to Pakistan as some of his antics had driven them up the wall. Some of these very walls he had daubed cryptic messages and crazy graffiti that the local crews had adopted as their own. Danny had skills - he would chat the same way to local prostitutes that he would chat to the Mayor or Police Sector Commander. But then he fell, after a group of the Councilllors finally snapped after he had exposed some dodgy planning application for yet another fried chicken establishment. They had said he had held a girl hostage in the old playground and after the Police helicopters had left the scene he had been led away and taken to Haleacre the local loony bin. Enough of the brothers together with the local youth worker had campaigned for his release but the men in white coats had taken him away. Life was never the same afterwards and even when he came back out for brief periods the fire in his eyes was lost and he wasn't the same Danny Raja. Pumped full of drugs he was too zonked out to have any perception of where he even was. Asif was sad when he died but he also knew that Danny had died that day the *Marvay* had picked him up. He had never seen so many peeps turn up to a funeral - two sixth forms closed and seven taxi companies shut up shop for that day (one base stayed open to mop up business and was subsequently boycotted and closed down in six months). Women were seen crying in the streets and little snotty kids hugged each other in recognition of what they had lost. Three junkies overdosed and half a dozen lads got married in the space of a month. Danny dying woke a lot of them up but their eyes and minds were not fully open enough for them to pick up his message and run with it. Maybe that would be asking too much and they all had dollars to make. But he lived on, fuelling booze and spliff filled nights where all the old stories would come out and cold hard pauses would meet the dawn with the slow realisation that they would have to get up and face the day without him.

1968: Life in Whitelands

It was all over town but Mohinder did not know why and in any case this was not his town or *shehar*. He stood by the poster with Hussain bhai outside their factory and asked him to read it as his *Angreezi* was better than his.

"Munda kaun hai?"

"Some politician *Sardar*, we better be careful" said Hussain as Mister Lloyd, one of the foreman at the factory where they worked walked past

"Your brown friend is right. If I were you I'd stay out of the centre of town that night. Isn't everyday that Enoch Powell comes to a place like Wycombe to speak at a public meeting and there are a lot of

English folk who support this gentleman. Unfortunately this will mean curtains for you guys and I'll have to look for other staff to cover the nightshift"

Both Hussain and Mohinder looked at each other wondering why the foreman would be giving them such a gift and then clocked out. They had become friends when Mohinder had jumped in when Hussain had a run in with some white youth on the High Street. News had got out subsequently that this particular Sikh immigrant had been a champion wrestler back home - 'in the Punjab' as one of the managers put it. Mohinder wondered if he was 'in the England' in the same way but the looks from some of these johnnies was hardly friendly. Hussain was going to bring his wife over but Mohinder was determined to go back even though he had been saying that every month since 1962. As they walked back to their rented housing in Castlefield Hussain explained what he had heard about Powell from family in the Midlands and the speech he had heard on the radio.

"Powell wants us out *yaara*"

Hussain would speak to him in a combination of *Pihar*i, Punjabi, Urdu and English. It did not matter about their respective faiths they could communicate and whatever happened right now he was his brother

"*Theek hai* we'll book our flights - I'll speak to my brother in law in Southall'

"I'm staying *yaar* - my wife is coming over next month. It took a year to save up the *paisay* and they're building that stupid dam so half my village will be coming soon. I have to buy a house'

"A house? You'll be lucky - who's going to lend money to a wog?'

"I'll sort it out brother - *dal roti* again tonight for me and you. Amjad's *salee* cooked again"

They kept walking with their heads down to avoid the cutting wind and any attention from those coming out of the pubs at this time. As he saw the sign for Whitelands Road he breathed a sigh of relief even though the name reminded him of his situation every day when he saw it.

Hussain did not attend the Labour Party meeting being held in Green St School - they had been leafleting outside the house on Jubilee Road they used for Friday prayers. He did not want trouble and from the leaflets that were being given out to support Powell he knew that there would be trouble even if he was only talking about Europe and free trade and not immigration. Anyway Mohinder was working that evening and he like most Asians in the town would not go anywhere on their own and definitely not to a meeting about someone like Powell. That would be asking for trouble and just being a brown skinned man in Buckinghamshire was enough right now.

Every so often Mohinder would go for a drink in the Saracen's Head on Green Street. A few Indian lads and the odd Pakistani could be found here with their West Indian brethren wiling away the hours. It was one of the few places that he knew he would get served pretty quickly and there were enough fellow blacks to watch his back. Hussain had come in a few times but when he saw a distant relative with a brandy in the corner he had decided to evade this particular drinking hole as the *goray* called it. Once he found out what a Saracen actually was he found it very funny that the pub was located so close to many Pakistani Muslim families. Hussain refused to believe him but once he read an article in the Bucks Free Press he conceded that a pub could be named from the times of the Crusades. Don't think it helped him that he started to carry his *Kirpaan* with him just in case they went for his neck. Even though he was not a Muslim he could understand the panic within his Pakistani brother's mind – they all wore their passports on their skins in these difficult times.

Patricia Shaw was waiting at the surgery, indeed she had been waiting for longer than she had anticipated due to a set of new immigrants registering. She could not understand what they were saying in their Hindustani gibberish but the odd word of English was heard and she wondered how long this would all last. The Wycombe that she knew was changing - the woods that had surrounded her life growing up around West Wycombe Road being replaced by more industrial units and housing and the local white working class now being scattered around and these new black and brown faces suddenly emerging. These were not the negro GI Joes stationed in the town during the war that she remembered seeing but Indian chaps and Caribbean men and women with blue lips and bad luggage. She wasn't a racialist by any means but she felt a sense of unease at the changes that she was saying. Perhaps that awful Mr

Powell was right and they had unleashed the River Tiber. Jonathan her son was now a year old and she wondered what kind of world he was going to grow up in.

Chapter Six

'The road is a word, conceived elsewhere and laid across the country in the wound prepared for it: a word made concrete and thrust among us.'

Wendell Berry

First the people came and then the paths. The paths created routes for the hamlets and small settlements and a way for livestock to travel up and down the sides of the valley. Before the roads came they were the only ways that people travelled between where they lived and also to the holy sites that existed. Then the mills and the markets came and the settlements became villages and the town grew larger. As roads were created some of the paths disappeared as the roads were built straight on them but others persisted to be the lifeline for travelers and a source of fear for some. Some paths were associated with thieves and groups of Highwaymen that had made the Chilterns their home. As the town grew bigger it was mainly the Bodgers working in the woods turning chair legs that would use these routes. As this too disappeared the use of the paths reduced but if you looked closely they were still there criss-crossing the town like a tapestry from the past indicating the ancient ways and lost settlements.

It always used to make him wonder. He hadn't noticed till now. It had been there at the back of Shiraz's mind nagging away but he'd never really thought it through till now:

A group of young Pakistani lads had been stopped recently in a vehicle with a number of baseball bats. Nothing unusual 'bout that - they were the weapon of choice for any respectable Asian man aged 18-25yrs and in possession of some kind of driving license. Occasionally you'd also come across the odd ceremonial swords. What was more unusual was that not only did they have the gloves and balls (a well known ploy) but they had pads and helmets. Well sadly the Officers panicked fearing that a serious ruck was brewing. It turned out that they were part of a West London Asian baseball team on their way to a fixture in Oxford. Of course they missed their game and it took some frantic calls to the US to even get them released after 48 hours. For some reason however it started a strange trend for baseball paraphernalia in High Wycombe. The interest in Mogul antique swords was a bit more obvious.

He'd been doing house to house visits around the vicinity of the skip where they found her. Sergeants and investigating officers had kept him at arm's length due to him being new to PCSO work but this was his manor and he knew that he could work the angles and get some info. He'd felt sorry for the bitch but as soon as he'd gone through her file at the station and got some details from the interviews it had all came together. She'd gone to the school up the hill. Another Grammar school reject wasting their life away at a lowlife school. Shiraz knew he was lucky he'd made it to Royal Grammar and whilst those were not the most comfortable of days for him he'd made it through. It was the sixth-form that had fucked him up. Passing his driving test and learning how to build a spliff had caused him to take a bit of 'time out' from school. In truth they chucked his arse out and even his well connected Pops could do nothing for him to get back in. But this girl was a classic case - another wayward daughter from an *unpurr* family.

There were bits of the town that Mandy sought refuge in, the older bits of High Wycombe that no one noticed anymore 'cos it had always been there. Those bits were going ever quicker. There were only a few places where a CCTV camera couldn't get to. Everywhere was covered by a lens now. The little Ayesha's and Nadeems were now having to find other places to kiss and fondle each other especially after the 'Samina' scandal - a bunch of local Councillors were being shown around the security suite/control room in the main shopping centre and the local managers was boasting about being able to watch something like 30 places at any one time. One particular camera was filming two brown skinned lovers in a car park one of whom was the daughter of one of these Councillors!

She looked at the time on her phone - yet again she was being stood up and kept waiting. Fuck 'em she thought if they can't turn up with her *maal* - her high grade, then she would go somewhere else. She grabbed her stuff and went to open the bedroom door. Her hand grabbed the handle of the door but it wouldn't give. The bastards had locked her in again. She went up to the window and saw the newly installed barbwire that the benevolent landlord Mister Khan had erected. He liked erections she'd heard but this one in particular had pissed her off big style. Mandy looked at her fist and smashed the window.

Shit was getting mad on the ground over Mandy's body. All of a sudden peeps were talking 'bout who did it and all kind theories were being propagated. Asif wanted to know, he wasn't sure why. Calling it revenge was too simple. There were too many questions floating about in his head, motives and what trouble she must have been in. He talked to her more in the few hours that he spent with her each week then he ever did with his Mrs. But she had never let on about her situation and he didn't want to ask as he accepted it all at face value. He would never have left his family for her and she was never gonna settle down to be a housewife and give up her day job. Both of them accepted the impasse they were in and their weekly love-ins were a bonus. Least they practiced safe sex and Asif would never had done the dirty like some of the brothers did - sleeping around without condoms and given their partners STI's. Some of these poor girls had ended up getting beats because suspicion would point at them rather than their husbands. Most of them ended up getting diseases they had never heard of and their hubbys couldn't even spell.

The yellow lines were wonky on West Richardson Street. Everyone could see that and yet no one did anything about it. Asif would park his car up in between pickups and try and catch sight of Mandy. During this time he would alternate between chatting to the Base and going through his wife's latest conversation with him.

"Where you goin'?"

"Out"

"Riswan's in trouble - he took a knife out on a teacher in class"

"Boys always do stoopid things"

"He's seven years old Asif - seven"

"I'll talk to him tomorrow"

"*Khub* Asif? You're always so tired when you get back from work"

"I pick him up Fridays - I'll speak to him"

"You should keep him away from your brothers"

"Jimmy and Fungus love him"

"They're teaching him bad ways Asif. You weren't there when he called Nargis Auntie a dirty ho"

"Ok ok I'll talk him"

"You better otherwise your son will be shifting kilos down Bowerdean"

At least he'll bring some money in he thought as his wife gave him that stern 'don't fuck with me' look. Man he hated it when she was right but he wasn't really the best kind of guy to be a father (or a husband come to think of it) He liked to stray away much too much.

Stacey desperately tried to stay awake during the Community press conference that had been called. The Police were struggling to get any information about Mandeep's murder and short of mounting a Crimewatch reconstruction they were facing a wall. Anyway in the scheme of things the death of a Sikh prostitute didn't warrant national coverage. Stacey may have been white but she wasn't naive to the ways of the world. She knew the youth workers on the panel were fairly knowledgeable but they didn't want to know her. Instead she was left picking up the crumbs from pervy Councillors who would not avert their eyes from her breasts. They would mouth the normal platitudes and then go home and beat their daughters. Their sons would continue to wolf whistle and kerb crawl with abandonment safe from harm. It wasn't that difficult for a Home Counties chick like her to understand. During the conference the cops were as cagey as ever and the Council Officers were a complete waste of time, unprepared to deviate from their scripts and just dished out the same old line. Most people were too busy just positioning themselves and trying to manage away the situation. The town wasn't the safest for women - the figures from Women's Aid were testimony to that. But as usual a bunch of white & brown blokes were completely oblivious to these facts.

She was trailing this taxi driver who'd been seen with her the night before for an interview. The other lead seemed to be some spurious link to a maverick white independent Councillor - who had gone through all the political parties and then set up his own neighborhood watch style rump that based it's rational on spying on the Asian community. Stacey was proud of the front cover story a few more like that and she would be sure that that one of the nationals would come crawling after her. Stacey prided herself on her investigative skills and the inside info she always managed to get. The murder had been tied into battles between taxi companies over lucrative fares for dealers and users. Many of the suppliers had got wise to driving smart motors due to constant surveillance and the taxi firms had moved in. The girl had been a witness to a argument that had morphed into a vicious assault which had led to a number of local hoods being put into comas. Mandy had been 'removed' and her death used as a warning sign. She had nailed the story, raised her profile and was one step closer to getting out of this town.

1977

'Zindagi ka yeh safar koi samjhe to nahin

Yehi rasta hai mera koi aata hi nahin'

'Khwaab' Niraj Chag

She wrapped up Asif in the blanket in the old buggy and set off back home. Only her cousin brother Younis had a car and Atia like many other women would put the shopping under the pram or on the handles of a buggy and walk home. England was always dirty grey like the slushy snow under her foot. Only early in the morning or on the hills on both sides did it stay white like the valleys in Mirpur. She would pass the many furniture factories and marvel at what was being made by the master craftsmen. Many of her husband's family were employed on the late shifts, sometimes working through the night at Barretts and Keens and just on the corner of the School by Green St they're had been a factory which had been demolished a few years back. The whole area had been the centre of the furniture trade many years ago her husband had said in those few moments he had talked to her. He had said the Britishers reckoned that it would be only be a few more years and then all the jobs would go – she wondered what he and all the others would do after that. The life he had of working shifts and playing cards in between would change. She had bigger plans for Asif – a good school and for him to go to University but she did not know what this town would bring for them all in the future.

The *Qayamat* Hotel

He had not stayed there for many years and when he had it had been a fleeting visit. He hadn't like the place and had just wanted to go home. Asif was not sure how this place had come to be, this destination that was never going to be found by a Sat Nav. Maybe it came to you after a trip back home or a particularly drunken night when you had pissed yourself on the landing or ended up at sleeping in a car. He did not know how it all had come about. All he knew was that he had good friends who resided there and he had lost all hope of ever being reuniting with them.

He had lost a friend once, but it had been a tragedy that had taken her. Bilkis had been 13 years old when she lost her Dad after an industrial accident in a warehouse up at Cressex. Till that point she had been his twin, his mirror image, his best spar and confidante. After her Dad died she stopped coming out and decided to go to Saudi to stay with her *Chachi*. When she came back Bilkis was no more and had been replaced by a devoutly religious young woman who had become narrow and conservative. It wasn't the burqa or her wanting to go to a girl's school that bugged him. It was just that she had decided then and there that in this new life that there was no space for any friendship with him. As he saw her around through the years she drifted into a world that Asif did not understand and with groups that saw Pakistani's like him as little more than *Kuffar.* She had told him to his face that he was not a proper Muslim and would suffer in the afterlife, but the children wrapped around her black voluminous gowns meant that there was no future for the both of them together whether he was devout or not. She was lost to him and increasingly inward looking and pious, and even the looks when she would pass by in the shops gave her away. As the junkies and the prostitutes increased Bilkis would continually warn people about the Day of Judgment and that *Qayamat* would descend on them all. She had checked in, she had her room key and there she would remain, in a bubble of her own making, against their lies and against his life. A better place, they were in a better place he would imagine. It was a state of mind for people who had resigned themselves to ever having control over their lives.

1913

Annie's family lived on 6 to 7 shillings a week and they were lucky if they had meat and milk most weeks. Her dad would moan about wage deductions as would have to pay for electric and his own tools. The only way they survived through the seasons was the home grown vegetables her Grandad grew on a little plot by his house. Her first memories if her childhood was her father taking her cherry picking in Flackwell Heath. When the fruit was in season half the town's families would converge in the woods to pick them. When she and her brothers and sisters grew tired they would take it in turns to ride in his board Limerick shoulders back to their small house in Newlands. Her father would then retire to the Golden Fleece public house and would disappear for a few days working and on Union business. He would surface tired and sweaty and invariably would get first dibs on the bath that was in the front room. Her father was a timid man who grew louder after the influence of a few pints and depending on the company around him. He looked like any Irish labourer in the town but if you put him in front of a crowd of workers he would roar like a lion against the oppression of his fellow people.

She stood at the back of the meeting and whilst there were some strong women who would air their grievances it was mainly the men folk who spoke and took the lead. Annie was impressed by Merthyr Molly who lived over in Micklefield with other Welsh families. Her husband had died in an accident at a furniture factory and she had never received support from the firm. The local union had helped her out and even though there were rumours about how friendly she was with some of the union officials Annie still had a deep admiration for her.

Chapter Seven

Shiraz threw the newspaper in the bin. That bitch of a journalist had gone front cover with the taxi gang link to Mandeep's murder. It was the hottest lead that they had but not all the evidence was there. Most of it was hearsay and gossip from deep within the bowels of the Pakistani community (so most of it was pretty shit). This would potentially screw up the investigation; inflame the situation and get people's backs up. She'd no doubt had a 'source' from within who'd leaked the story - a copper looking for some extra dosh or most likely some in-fighting between seniors. Either way it was a PR disaster which would mean him having to spend more time in Taxi bases chatting crap to his distant Uncles.

A few weeks into the new job Shiraz had put his name down for as many in-service training programs that Sarge would let him get away with. Initially he had done it to avoid pounding the streets, the circuit training that was going out on a bike and the depressing conversations that he had with his partner in the patrol car about the lack of her sex life. But at some point it had dawned on him that he was actually taking stuff in. Today's session was on grooming - now Shiraz had heard of this going on and he knew that it had nothing to do with farm animals or your pet dog like the jokers at the back of the group had pointed out. He'd found it quite sickening the more he learnt about grooming techniques and how men used their power to control young women. The worst thing was that he'd seen all the signs before being rehearsed by would be pimps and lowlifes in front of him in his area. He'd seen it being done in front of him and he'd colluded with it by saying or doing nothing. Shiraz would have to live with the *sharam* but he knew the course would help him get ahead - make him a proper copper one day or even make CID. He knew he had to stay focused.

Something always drew Mandy to trouble. Maybe it was *kismet* or she was a victim of circumstance. She seemed to spend a lot of time in empty rooms. Akky had been sweet at first and then slowly he started being a shit, introducing her to his friends

"Just go wit him Mandy. Look it's jus' a paisa ting I need to settle up and I'm short dis month"

He would give a smile and she would see herself reflected in his gold tooth. She would submit to his will and take some dick. But those were the good days, least they would meet up at night to blaze and then eat chicken wings with his sister. Yea it seemed strange chilling with her but when she found it was family concern and that she was just a franchise for one of the brothers it made her sick to her stomach. But by then it was too late for her and she just accepted whatever came her way.

Life could be a blur sometimes. She would be stuck in the same routines and each punter would pretty much look the same. Some days she would reminisce about her school days and the stupid conversations she had with her mates about boys. Asif hadn't existed then, he'd been in class with her but seeing him as a sexual being had not been on her radar. He was just another Pakistani boy with perspiration problems and abnormal facial hair. He hadn't seen her either and to most of them she was just another *sikhnee* but at the same time he had not stood out as relationship material. Girls on the other hand were friends and competitors. At her school you had to watch your back 'cos girls could hurt you and inflict serious pain. Her crew was safe but there were always beefs and arguments that needed to be settled one time. Mandy had tricks, she knew the runnings and she would laugh at the girls who got played time and time again. She had been sharp at school but was not particularly academic and once she was on her own she learnt how to survive.

Asif stood in the car park on West Richardson Street and inhaled deeply from his cigarette. You could see both sides of the valley from here. See the million pound houses going to the M40 and then there was the dump that he lived in just round the corner. Seven of them in a three bed terrace. His wife and kid, his mum and dad - increasingly senile and demanding, and his younger brother & sister always at each other's throats and always lying through their teeth. He had long stopped worrying about them and though Shakila was covered now and Babar had grown a beard he knew they were up to stuff. Who was he to judge? He'd been the same and probably a lot worse. He was just glad that Jimmy & Fungus his older brothers were in and out of nick doing short sentences for one thing or another.

He scratched his goatee and wondered where Mandy was. It was their usual time and she hadn't shown. Her phones were dead and she wasn't at the flat. If she was down the clinic she would have told him. Asif continued to stare out this time looking up and down the valley impatiently. So much stuff was going down right now - the bigger truth was that it wasn't just about the brown part of town, there were peeps from everywhere who had a handle on this bullshit. White boys from the estates, mixed race crews and *kalay* all with an axe to grind or some beef to sort out. You throw the Polish into the mix and things were screwed. Worst of the worst were the middle-class *goray* and their *chumchay* who presided over all this - who let stuff happen, turned a blind eye and let things go 'cos their brothers/uncles/nephews were involved. He had thought about moving to Marlow or Princes Risborough but when he had seen the house prices he had quickly changed his mind. He may have been sitting in a crock of shit but at least he knew the runnings. He flicked the fag end away and jumped into the Zafira.

He turned around the car and went past the police station again. The Saab was a smooth but meaty vehicle and he managed the maneuver quickly glancing at the mirror to see how further grey and thin his hair had become. The silver mane was in decline, maybe just like the cause he was deeply submerged in. There was a group of protesters outside the police station. He could see a small banner and some placards with a picture of a half caste man with dreadlocks. The hit on this particularly despicable character had been successfully carried out by one of his associates in a custody setting. It looked as if he had family & friends who actually cared which was quite unusual. They mostly removed the detritus that was unwanted and on the margins. It looked like he had children from several partners who gave each icy looks whilst still in grief and anger. He parked up in the council car park and put on a pair of aviators and observed the scene. It was obvious the miscreant had a few friends from the criminal classes - the small gathering included assorted drug dealers, junkies and prostitutes that were common in these supply chains. A few bemused police officers were in attendance - vigils and political activity of this kind were virtually unknown in this sleepy town and the odd death or two and beatings administered by the police deemed as acceptable by the masses. He spotted a few troublesome activists who were always sniffing around and who were quick to point the finger at the police and authorities. The urban ecosystem was a delicate one. He had been trained to make skilled interventions but was still amazed at the consequences and how the dominoes would fall and the impact that this would have on the lives of others and in the very landscape itself. The only certainty was in the roads and rivers in the town but even these could be altered and covered up. The tracks would fade in time but the actions would linger, fester and multiply. From chaos there would be order.

Shiraz kept running into the journalist – at every step she seemed to be there and their run-ins were beginning to annoy him:

"You're a bit young to be a copper"

"You're a bit young to be a journalist and getting yourself mixed up in stuff you don't understand"

"So you got an insider's view then?"

"Don't try and poke around I ain't your normal Mirpuri softhead"

"You reckon you'll get a proper badge out of this then, use the girl's death to get yourself a promotion?"

"Same way you write shit to sell papers. Who's doing the using?"

"Maybe we can help each other..."

"....So both of us benefit and we walk away happy?"

"Yea that's what I'm proposing"

"No I don't buy it and I don't trust you. You've told lies in your reports, twisted facts around and you expect me to trade info with you"

"Look I can write it up so you're the fucking hero you get me?"

"Except there are no clear leads it's just all speculation. That's not gonna interest you is it? The same gossip I picked up you've probably picked up. You definitely get around"

"Don't need the sexist undertones Officer"

"Don't play the innocent. We know how you work. There are a dozen brown hands jerking off to you every day. You are a popular lady down Lindsay Avenue"

"Funny"

"I will find out who killed her. I owe it to my people and yea I wanna be CID someday and if this helps then fine. Just keep out of my way, this is serious business going down and you could get hurt"

"I'm glad to know you care so much about me"

"I don't, but I don't fancy finding your body in a skip...."

The bitch was getting to him. Yes he found her sexy 'cos she had a brain and unlike some of the brown sisters in town was obtainable and in his reach. Only his principles and distrust was stopping his cock from rising. There were too many blocks in his head and his own blatant ambitions. Only he could find the killer and he didn't need no *goree* hack screwing it up.

He walked off and she wanted to scream. She just wanted to do her job - she didn't need this shit from a PCSO. The guy wasn't even a proper copper. She would stay tight to him - dig a little and find out if he had cousins that would talk. Stacey was not going to let this story go. She had invested too much time and energy on Mandy.

By the time Asif got home his dinner had got cold & and his wife had gone missing. Mum was visiting some relatives up north & he was too lazy to go warm anything up. He wasn't a complete waste of time in the kitchen - he had been known to make a cup of tea & toast but he saw his role to bring the money in to buy the food rather then make it himself. Maybe it was a backward point of view but he was hardly moving forwards. The executive chauffeuring was dying a death as many of the big corporates and blue chip companies were moving their contracts to firms who had less Muslim drivers on their books. Apparently the executive types were getting a bit nervous & sweaty around the brothers. Asif had always prided himself on his *gora* banter but now he was wasting his days chatting to his no good uncles at the taxi base and missing his dinner. He stared towards the direction of the kitchen and rang up for a pizza.

Mandy hated the way that they stared at the bodies going past. It wasn't just the Asian taxi drivers; the Kashmiri crews and their new South Indian 'brethren'. From her various vantage points she would see a wide variety of men eyeing up school girls, breasts like pimples coming home at half past three, the local slappers who would seemingly spend all day in the bus station, to the white men fantasising bout a scarf covered girl & even those in full niqab. This would mainly revolve around their sad fantasies of what they wore underneath. The cold hard stares that many of the white girls had to endure with the cheeky 'are you up for it' grins that some of the Asian younger lads gave made her feel sorry for them. Of course this quickly evaporated when they opened her mouth in her direction. Her position as the sole brown girl operating was not to be envied. Mandy hated the way they would tease her & use her against Asian punters. Maybe they didn't want an Indian every night 'cos that is what they got at home she would say. She knew that this would mean in the main some *roti* & *choosa* rather than the other but occasionally their barbed comments would get to her - not that she would show it on her face. Life is in the other bodyshop was hard & no one ever came out smelling gorgeous.

1913

Anna could see her brother being struck by the truncheon but she was powerless to stop it, it was only when an Anti-Violence Brigade volunteer stepped in that the police backed away. Annie did not just fear the police she despised them and to her labourer Dad and brothers they were little better than the scabs they shipped in when they locked the workers out of the factories they worked in. It was lucky that the hefty AVB fella was there as the copper would have got a beating.

Her family on her Mum's side had been bodgers for two generations until the factories opened and everyone flooded to the town. Their house on Baker Street housed five people and Annie was grateful as some had more. She'd grown up playing in Oakridge Woods but now like the other girls she was being prepared to be a Caner, putting together the final bits of a chair before it was sold. This was a career destination for many women this side of the town. They made some fine chairs but they would never sit on them - that pleasure would be for the well to do's on West Wycombe Road or up Amersham Hill. Annie resented the rich in the town almost as much as she hated the police.

Chapter Eight

The place was a shithole of the highest order. It reeked of piss and ammonia mixed in with a large dose of Stella. Shiraz had been called out with PC Saminah Khan to some old warehouse building off the industrial park. Place was stuck in time. He could never work out why these places were left standing while the rest of town was getting shiny new shopping centres and being regenerated. Shiraz wasn't even sure why he had been sent here. It was only Saminah's presence that made it worthwhile - she was pretty hot for a Kashmiri girl with a headscarf. He did have respect for her though. It turns out she had to really fight her folks to be a copper. Even though both her mum and dad were educated it had been a real battle. Her pops was even some Diversity and Equal Opportunities Advisor to the local FE College. Thinking about it though, even that was no guarantee of support. In the end she did it and turned out to be the first homegrown female Asian copper from the town. So Shiraz was not only attracted to her but was slightly in awe. Not that it mattered right now as he waved great white streaks of cobwebs off his face:

"We got reports that groups of young Asian men are congregating here"

"Well there is a bus stop just on the corner"

She would stare at him intently when he cracked these stupid jokes.

"PCSO Ali I need you to follow up a request that was made regarding a particular group. Do you have a problem with that?"

"No sir"

"Go with PC Khan - she knows the industrial estate"

Maybe he had a problem dealing with authority or that this sergeant had a complex 'bout brown people. He just felt that he was getting cut out of the Mandy case. His local knowledge was backfiring on him. One of the Officers felt he was too close to the incident. His new life as Police Community Support Officer was an eye opener for him as he went through room by room in the crappy warehouse cursing the bastards who sent him there.

"Why are we here Sammy?"

She looked at him and her nose twitched in a way that Shiraz found most pleasing

"PCSO Ali we're following orders and can I just remind you that I am your Probationary officer in this instance"

So that's how you want to play he thought. *Chal larkee* we'll play it your way

"I'm sorry PC Khan but I can't see the relevance to the Hothi murder"

"We follow every lead we are told to follow - these old buildings are used by all sorts of criminal elements and we may find some evidence that links us to the crime"

She talked like a police manual and there was no way she was going to let him in. All he could do was admire her glacial efficiency from afar.

She would sit on her own in between sitting on guys faces and think about her school days. She'd think about all of those kids and what they were up to. Mandy had kept in touch with a few but most had disappeared into the ether – ending up in prison, married or dead or some weird combination of the three. People made their choices and either regretted it or paid for it with their lives. She, she was in some next world, constantly sparking up, shooting up or getting horizontal. The two blokes banged her and left. She lit a spliff and put it to one side and found the brown. She started her normal routine and then she thought another client had turned up. Mandy looked out the window and saw an elderly white gentleman dressed very smartly in some Volvo estate. She didn't think much of it and got back to business - she had four hours to kill.

Mandy had been talking to some of the Polish girls who had started. When she had heard their stories she had felt quite guilty and humbled. They had been tricked into coming here under the pretence that they were secretarial supply staff and then forced to go on the game by elusive gang masters. They were pretty and white and fresh meat for the men folk of Wycombe. Nobody gave a shit about them UK sides and they had no family locally. Mandy would try and translate for them as she'd picked up a few polish phrases especially when they went for medical checks at the clinic but she never interfered with anything else. Their minders had a reputation for violence and would indulge in vicious beatings when the mood took them and she was not that brave to try and take them on.

Mandy was tired and put her head down on the yellowing pillow case and closed her eyes. She grabbed the air on her descent and passed the hills those green and white chalk hills that she had stared at when she had been on father's shoulders. Those strong board shoulders that had carried her away from the market and back to her home. His *pagri* tapping on her thighs and his deep bassy voice filling the air with rustic folk songs. She felt herself sink deeper and deeper into sleep.

Stacey was waiting in the town. What was up with this guy? He said he would meet her in the car park on Westbourne St. He had been linked with Mandy and some of the other drivers had said she had had a thing for him. Asif somebody his name was - all these taxi drivers seemed a blur to her now.

He drove in and parked up and Stacey got out and got into the silver Zafira. He decided to take her up to Hughenden.

"Did you and Mandy come up here?"

He didn't answer and thought about why she was asking him. He knew at that point it had been a mistake to take up her invitation.

"Well did you?"

"I'm a married man - what do you want me to say?"

"Look I won't mention it in the story"

"You stitched up Enzo"

"But he was shifting kilos from the back of his Dad's Italian restaurant"

"Let's just say I went to school with her"

"I don't think people want to know that, they want something juicier"

He started the engine up.

"I think you got the wrong person - sorry for wasting your time"

She said nothing more to him and he dropped her off by Argos

What was up that night with Mandy he would never ever know now. She had miscalled him and they had met and done their normal business. She'd been restless though and he had known it wasn't the drugs talking. He asked her if she was in trouble or if the boys had been roughing her up. Mandy point blank denied anything and just changed the subject. He'd got close to her and sometimes she felt she was his only real friend. In return he felt obliged to look out for her. Asif dropped her off to her mates and had gone to the Base. Three days later they found her body in a skip. He had failed in his duties.

He kept staring at the newspaper, then looked up to see Bash and Mangy scoring off some Polish geezer. He stared back at the headline and to her picture: "Taxi gangs killed Asian prostitute" Boxes of text gave details and interviews with ex school friends, some cousin from Slough and that prick of a Police Community Support Officer Shiraz Ali who had found her body. None of these people wanted to know her when she was alive and now she was dead here they were all pontificating beautifully. He slumped onto the wheel until his Auntie went past with her customary shopping bags and tapped on the window:

"*Teek ho*?"

He nodded and drove off before she went into one of her diatribes and got him to give her a lift. Which he did most of the time mainly to get rid of her but today was not one of these days. Memories of Mandy were still in his head. He drove up to the top of West Wycombe hill where he unzipped himself and wanked to her memory.

Stacey was now regularly getting the threats - letters on her landing and phone calls to her landline and mobile. Kiranjit her flat mate had laughed it off but even she was getting scared. Of course she didn't get was going on. She was the wrong kind of Asian to understand the situation that Stacey was going through.

"Just change the phone line Stace"

"They know where I live Kaz"

"You better move out then"

"I'll deal with it, get some advice of one of my Dad's solicitors"

Then the threats started to get vicious and they were describing what they were going to do to her. The police had tried to be helpful but they were pretty much useless. She was starting to get paranoid and screwed up.

"Can't you do something about the letters?"

She had asked the female Police Officer on her phone.

"It's all been recorded but we haven't got the Officers on the ground to be watching your place. I've arranged a police vehicle to swing by once a day to drive past but that's all that I can offer I'm afraid."

She'd hung up and lit a cigarette. She's smoked for three months in 2003 to impress a boy she fancied at College but this recent habit was bugging her. Cops were useless, she thought about contacting that Shiraz again but his last rejection was still ringing in her ears.

The Ruse

It was a ruse, a trick on a massive scale that only a few conspiracy fixated Black net heads had ever speculated on. Even then these blinkered African & Asian cultural nationalists were far too off the mainstream political landscape to gather any notice. A few had hinted at but never guessed the scale of social engineering that was going on. Only a blessed few on their side would pick on the occasional cryptic clues left in the slipstream. He hated these leftists with a vengeance. He hated the language they had constructed to define his kind. At various times they had been referred to as the 'New' Right & the 'Far' Right. He wanted to show these commentators that what he & his fellow officers were engaged in was not new & they were definitely not far away in that sense. The movement prided itself in having people placed in all echelons of life but in particular positions of power. Where there was safety they could reveal some aspects of their ideology without giving away details. He was well aware of the power of anti-fascist groups to try & infiltrate. They were lucky that most people had them pegged as merely Nazi hunters but he knew they could do significant damage. The lie was powerful - it had wrapped itself over the Chiltern Hills and the fabric of the County. It was embedded into the DNA of the mighty and the powerful and covered up a multitude of sins committed by them.

His role was minor but still significant - he was not concerned about which deputy mayor had been found with his trousers down in a local primary school. Despite the media reporting this having occurred in the staff toilets and being a 'lavatory accident' he knew that removing the stain upon this particular individual would be a stiff task. He was not concerned about private developers sitting on land on parts of the deprived areas of Chepping Wycombe as he still referred to the place. The trick being that they would wait for things to explode and do business with the highest bidder. The ironic fact being that these developers were buying land to stop development not to cause it and to stop another company from getting their own hands on it. Of course to lubricate this process all manners of curries & canapés were consumed. Illicit meetings and dodgy dealings were the order of the day. But it was not his job to get involved with these machinations he was a merely a removal man of the highest order.

Chapter Nine

Asif drove around the town like madman. The rain dropped down like a dark plague across the valley. Everywhere he went it went. He would get out at to all the spots that she would be in - behind the garages chatting to the Kashmiris just off the boat, the back of Tuck-In Cafe where a tired old boozer remained triumphant over a shiny new shopping complex which towered over it. He went down the Rye where the swings were full of flirting thirteen year olds. He went everywhere but no sign of her. Time was ticking away and he knew he would have to face up to the truth.

His wife stared at him with contempt:

"The car broke down. I got soaked"

"You had it serviced last week Asif"

"The car's our livelihood - it does bare miles *jaan*"

He tried her with the "*jaan*". Normally it could get him a reprieve, some breathing space and even a rare opportunity to get horizontal. But this time she stared straight through him.

"I'm at your mums with Riswan, and then I'm going out with Saiqa, *choosas* in the oven. I made the bed for you downstairs"

With that last sentence she slammed the door and the emptiness that would have to be filled now that Mandy was gone just glared at him. He went to the shed found some gear and booze he had stashed away and built up a big zoot. He grabbed a bottle of rum and settled down in front of the TV. Opposite the sofa was nicely made up as a bed. As he snuggled underneath the duvet he recalled the conversation that he'd had with the PCSO Ali:

"You asked to see me?"

"I got to speak to you about Mandeep Hothi – Mandy"

"She meant nuthin' to you when she was alive why you bothering now"

"My sister knew her. Anyway I'm a copper now it's my business to know"

"Your sisters were snobs – they looked down on everyone 'cos they were from Pindi. You think you're a big man now. You ain't a proper copper – you're fuckin' part time. You can't even nick me"

"You wanna test me on that one bruv?"

"I'm not yer bruv Shiraz. Me and you parted ways long way back so don't give me that bruv shit!"

"You're pretty high & mighty for a taxi-driver"

"I don't do taxi's no more I do executive chauffeuring"

He'd left it there and walked away. Asif had some had some serious backup and he didn't fancy a run in right now or a showdown in Bridge Street car park. He had a hunch there was a link to Mandy but he knew if he pursued it that he would be in some deep shit. It did not pay to mess with taxi drivers even when they were doing executive chauffeuring...

Shiraz was a prick and so up himself. What was it with Pakis with a badge or a uniform or even these illiterate council *wallay* who would prostitute themselves in the town hall? Shit was messed up. He'd backed down of course which was a strange thing for him to do. A few years ago he would thought nothing of ringing the boys and making the wanker pick his teeth up from the floor. But he was a suspect now and however estranged he felt from his missus he had a responsibility to her and Riswan. Too many kids were getting used to see their *Abbos* in prison and he was determined to stay straight. He got to his car and seeing a few drops of petrol underneath it opened up the bonnet. The smell of petrol always reminded him of scooters in Mirpur town. Smoke and fumes were a regular part of living in any town or city in Pakistan. A bigger *shaher* like Karachi was even worse - not that he had been there. The largest city he had visited was Islamabad and even that had been an experience especially when he saw an army van hit a donkey in front of him on the outskirts of the city. His Chacha's moped had been covered in blood as the poor animal bled to death - he had been sitting behind his uncle and had been spared the immediate spectacle but the flecks of crimson blood had left his mark on him.

Stacey's childhood had been idyllic and even her parents' divorce hadn't rippled the waters. Both of them had done everything amicably and she and her older brother Jonathan had spent their teenage years in two houses with no ill effect. As she grew older she had found out that only a minority of parents actually stayed together and most of her friends were in the same boat. Her first memories involved being in some plush resort in Santorini, she was sure her Mother had said it was called Firostefani. It had been the palm trees and the Indonesian maids that had stuck in her head.

From a young age Stacey knew that her life meant something and that she was someone who was going to amount to something. Her Dad had said to her once that every generation needed 'movers and shakers' and she was determined to make her life meaningful and with purpose. Yea she wanted the money but most of all she craved the spotlight and adulation. Stacey wanted her own byline, a regular column and to enter that world based on her own skills rather than having to sleep her way to the top. Mum had said to Stacey once that she didn't have a silver spoon in her mouth she had a cutlery drawer. The enormity of this statement didn't make sense until she was in her late teens and floating through University. Mum's family were originally from Ireland and had made good from the furniture business in the town. In the space of two generations they had gone from being lowly bodgers to factory owners with the likes of the Skulls and Bartletts. Once they acquired more land and assets the family were rolling in it and her Mum had gone to prestigious schools in the area. She had grown up with a maid and any Irishness in her including her accent was knocked out of her within a few years and she prospered to become a beautiful Buckinghamshire lady with all the opportunities to make her way in the world. For Stacey it was only her Durham University days that had woken her up to the extent of her white privilege. Even then it was not something that she worried herself about. Her received pronunciation opened doors for her and even in the North East of England it was clear where she and her kind were meant for:

"Greatness Stacey, your generation will achieve everything that mine didn't"

Her Mum would say dropping hints that her choice of journalism would not be lucrative but would still enable her to reach great heights.

"There's still a glass ceiling Mother there's still not that many women execs in the media industry and only a handful in positions of power"

Stacey had interjected once. Remembering the talk some feminist journo had given at her University.

"You will break that darling and they'll be women media moguls mark my words"

Stacey didn't want to talk about the hard work this all involved let alone the sex and seduction involved. She knew plenty of women who did not have to open their legs to get ahead but she also knew that in the business she was going into sexual harassment was a reality and sometimes you either gave in or you gave up.

Asif struggled with it sometimes, sometimes it would weigh on him like the responsibility he had for his aging parents. Occasionally it would eat him up and he would simmer with anger. Most of the time he just coped - he was good at doing that, good at sweeping his thoughts away. He tried to blank out what she would be doing with her clients and that some of the people he knew had gone with her. He would never say anything to her and she would never talk about her customers. It was a place they were never to visit and a dark hole from which if ventured down they could be no return. As he read through the local rag he came across story about a gang fight. The swordfights were definitely not clever - in the age of CCTV, Neighbourhood Watch and rival families all ready to shop lads in it was really a no brainer. However every so often the situation would erupt at a street level and all manner of weapons would be produced. The made in China machetes were particularly popular with the lucky import/exporter responsible spotting a gap in the market for weapons designed to scare and inflict pain in equal measure. Asif had come close to a silver machete blade slicing an ear off in a particularly nasty incident involving a woman and her irate husband after which he had vowed to stay knife free. However his flirtations with women continued because he could largely not help himself as infidelity unfortunately was hard wired to his genes. Pops had an affair, well several, when he was a young boy and there was

at least one or two step brothers and sisters that he would be
uncomfortably introduced to at bigger family gatherings. All his
Dad's flings were with white women so they were a mixture of chavs,
reverts and born again Pakistanis. When he was younger he was not
impressed and felt sorrow and loyalty to his *Ammi*, but as he grow
older and cynical about what he could get from life he took anything
that was going.

Street Corners

It was Baba's corner, that's how she knew it. Mandeep had always
seen him there either sitting or standing. His windswept chiseled
features were hewn into his face like the old council building behind
him. He never bothered anyone and hardly ever said a word. Smokes
would get passed around and every day the shopkeeper in the pet
shop would make him a cup of tea & bring it out and the owner of the
Tuck Inn would sneak him a plate of chips. In her circle Baba was a
bit of a hero - he had taken on a Kashmiri taxi driver who had
slapped a mixed race girl who was touting on the main road. He was
always giving girls on the corner signals if cops were around or if
plain clothes were on duty. *Marvay* hated him & had tried every legal
process to move his arse from his spot.

He never talked to his Uncle anymore. Chacha had taken to drink in
his 40's after he was made redundant in a local furniture factory and
his wife & kids had gone back to Mirpur. Everyone called him Baba
now and he inhabited a corner of Desborough road which was pretty
much his own *kotee*. He was part of the furniture of the streets and

as much part of the mythology of the terrain that Danny Raja had been. He seemed to be at peace with himself & was now off the wagon but seemed to more comfortable on the pavement and the kerb than in an old people's home. Asif still looked out for him, as did half the street but always wondered what was going on in his mind.

Stacey was desperate - nothing new was coming out about the story. She had seen him on the corner & she was sure that he had seen her as new face on the scene. Nothing had registered with him & he had stared through her as if she was not there. When she flashed a note to him and put it on his palm he looked at her & returned it. She found out later that his name was Baba & he was mentally ill so he was no use to her or the story. Another hour had been wasted and it was drifting away from her. There were no other openings apart from the one eyed minicab driver who eyed her up at the train station and they had got chatting - he had some angles that were worth pursuing. Contrary to received opinion Stacey hadn't slept around. Nowadays her sex life had taken a back seat & she was too busy chasing guys with long beards who had short stories to tell. For her the whole coming of age rituals had been a letdown & full of bad memories of kissing guys with vomit on their breath and sperm stains on the backseat of the car. She wasn't naïve - sex was a weapon that she could deploy it was just the actualities that were off putting. Her last partner had been some sorry arse record company exec who she'd got rid off after he'd asked to wear an adult sized nappy in her company.

Baba was a joke. Yea he was old enough to be his Uncle but he had never brought into that silent but wise man routine. He was a proper wino, maybe you didn't see him with a bottle in his hand anymore but Shiraz knew his game. Yea he knew Babar Rehman was 49 years old and had a number of convictions to his name. He read his file on the police computer & had played footie with his nephew. There was nothing too surprising about his story either - yet another middle age Pakistani man going to pot. Funnily enough his kids were doing well in Lahore but there was no contact anymore with them or his ex wife.

He had to work out all the angles, check the temperature and make the cut. For him it meant assessing the situation with the various warring factions/villages/taxi firms. If you then threw in postcodes and Island/Yardie affiliations and newly arrived Eastern European groupings it was an incestuous mess. Incestuous as many of these groups would have close links and even intermarry or at various times there would be truces of one kind or another. He surveyed the old man on the street corner and assessed his usefulness. He had seen enough of this Baba character to realize that he was a bit part player in the scheme of things but not valuable enough for him to warrant further attention.

The Assassin's missions would include observing the interesting street characters that inhabited the town of which Baba was one of many. He did not appear to have any value but was aware that he too had a watching brief and he still needed to be careful. Every so often he would book a taxi to take him from Wycombe to Chesham or from Aylesbury to Amersham. Each time he would use a different taxi company in those towns. He would engage in conversations with the drivers who would reveal a great deal about their lives and general maneuverings they had to make. No one ever asked him questions - an elderly wealthy distinguished gentleman did not stand out and as long as he paid the fare and a tip no one raised his existence. Occasionally he would come across other operatives in the field but apart from a knowing glance there would be no rapprochement. They were no quaint masons club or even a dodgy secret society. All contact was at a minimum and always through agreed channels only; a deep cover to conceal their actions.

Chapter Ten

'Life is one big road with lots of signs. So when you're riding through the ruts, don't complicate your mind. Flee from hate, mischief and jealousy. Don't bury your thoughts, put your vision to reality. Wake up and live!'

Robert Nestor Marley

1985

The bass line pumped through the building and the vibrations could be felt through the bricks of the Multiracial Centre. The sound system was tight with a group of lads hanging around the bins and the MCs chatting the night away. Different corners of the hall were full of people that represented the different faces of the town. There were the original Micklefield rude boys who loved their Ska and Rock Steady, a group of dreads from Castlefield and some crustie students with their roll ups and rings in their noses. In the corner there were a group of young Pakistani lads from Totteridge and

Green St with their St Vincent girl friends and a brave young bespectacled Asian man with skinny dreadlocks. The night was firing and would go down in the annals of the town's urban history. Wasn't every night that Jah Shaka and David Rodigan come to town and with local up and coming DJ Adrian Sherwood on selection duty this was always going to be a legendary night at the Multi.

The boys in the Anchor were not happy. The arrival of coach loads of Caribbean party goers was always going to incite them. As soon as news had spread about the show the gangs came together to tool up and meet up at their favoured drinking hole. Those cowardly National Front pricks bailed out and it was going to be left to the chosen white vanguard to protect the town from these black invaders. It was these wayward groups of mods, rockers and skins that would confront the police that were swarming around to protect these niggers and pakis that had congregated at the Multi. The presence of white people who sucked up to these foreigners was dutifully noticed and names written down for future fights. The student types were pussies but the rude boys who sided with the blacks were known for their fighting ways.

2007

Shiraz never found anything amusing about Amusement arcades but the kids did and he knew then that this would be somewhere he would need to check, to patrol. There would always be some kind of tricks going on and all manners of lowlife plying their trade. He'd been there once, on the fringes of it all as a Grammar school boy with his pockets full of coins for the machines, the Caribbean lads with white girls on their tails, always on their tails and the rest of the Asian boys with their bum fluff *muchay* and dodgy sideburns.

He had been told to sit in the cafe opposite and that's what he did – occasionally looking up from his Blackberry to check if the two lads he was looking out for had returned and he would regularly see that *goree* journalist reading some big arse newspaper or tapping on a phone. Mostly he would try and check any fit girls who would wander in or wander by. It was true that most of the Asian girls who he would be checking would be related to him one way or another. In a town like Wycombe you couldn't fart down one end without the other end complaining. Occasionally his mind would drift and he would think about the failed relationships in his life. He used the word 'relationship' very loosely as some of them had been dodgy encounters involving empty houses and vacant girls but there had been a few that were worth reminiscing about and of course there was still the question of his current supervisor:

PC Saminah Khan was fit.

It was an indisputable fact. Whatever angle you wanted to look at she was fit. To Shiraz it was all about the high Kashmiri cheekbones and fair Bollywood like skin that he always fell for. Together with the glacial frosty air that she would exude there was no doubting her formidable beauty. Formidable cos she could also beat your arse as she was not only a fourth Dan in Taekwondo but also held the record for a female PC completing the rigorous outdoor police training regime in the shortest amount of time. Every way you looked at it she was fitness personified. Shiraz had initially tried the polite chit chat that he saw *goray* around him use but she had batted this off like Mohammed Yousaf in his prime. Any direct attempt to chat her up led to him being reminded of his lowly position as a PCSO and that she was his probationary officer as well as the well worn routine that she was not that 'kind of *larkee*' . To Shiraz she managed the whole Muslim WPC role with amazing efficiency reflected in the neat niqab she wore. Don't think he had ever seen a hair out of place or it become disturbed. It remained tight and transfixing on her head whatever the weather or conditions. Her professional guard always stayed up and he had never seen her relax or let it down even in the staff room after hours or when she changed into her trendy trouser suit. He both admired and lusted over her most days but knew that it would never be a viable path for him to follow. That particular road was closed off with warning signs and police tape.

One day she would die in this town. Deep down Mandy knew it and the mirrors in the bus station confirmed her date with destiny. She looked a mess today and no amount of No7 was going to make a difference. Her tights had laddered and she could not be bothered going into New Look to get some more especially with the letchy bisexual security guard there who would flirt with anything in skirt, trousers or *shalwar kameez*. She sat down to light a cigarette and stared at the old people getting on and off buses. There was a particular hour in the day when it would mainly be elders and she wondered if that would ever be her with her free bus pass and sagging tits. It was approaching twilight and Mandy was trapped in the Desborough darkness and there were no routes open to her to get out.

This place could be any place he thought when the night came down and cast it's pallor on the valley. This place could be anywhere - the orange coloured streetlights bouncing off the cars and puddles on the pavements. The night would bring with it its fair share of lowlifes and street characters, shadows of people that would emerge when most were indoors watching reality TV whilst all the time hiding from it. There would be the crackheads Bash and Mangy on the corners, the four foot gangsters Kas and his crew breaking the windows of the Community Centre and little Marie, the fair skinned black girl selling herself on West Richardson Street. Maybe the people were the same too, different faces and postcodes but the same journeys being made and the same endgame. He'd see people coming out of the *Masjid* at prayer time and walk past all these characters to get to their cars. The Baptist would finish its charity evening to help the poor and its congregation would walk nervously to their own vehicles. Maybe they were all oblivious to it - he was sure that he was not the only person who could see what was going on. It could have been anywhere, any place but it wasn't - it was Asif's turf/area/*alaaka* and things were screwing up bit by bit like the dripping tap in the toilet that he couldn't fix 'cos he was too embarrassed to admit he couldn't change a washer. The drip drip was getting too regular now and he knew he would have to get Mad Waj to come and have a look at their plumbing situation. All the other stuff he had no answers for and he would just have to try and keep his own shit together. God knows that was hard enough. Bash, Mangy, Kas and Marie could screw themselves for all he cared and I suppose that they wouldn't need his help to manage that either.

He'd gone to do *avsoos* for Mangy's brother Iftikar who'd died from an overdose and been to the funeral in Wycombe's titchy little *Kurbistan*. Guy had been 21 and the dickhead had been injecting brown. It was only coming back and seeing the faces of the boys that had gone to school with him that the *unna* had dropped. Peeps were dying, some physically under the soil beneath his feet but some were dead and still walking around, cheating, robbing, fucking up their families and still pretending that 'tings were safe'. They were dead to the world, of any feeling and he hated them with every cell in his body. They would try and jump into his cab and get lifts through knowing his uncle or stating that they were from the same village back home. But he wasn't the kind of guy to get played and would take the small mini baseball bat that he kept hidden under his seat and bash a few heads. Next time he saw them they would look down, their yellowing faces hidden by a crusty hoodie. He had no time to feel sorry for them - he had a living to make.

This place was his place and he was tied here by an umbilical cord that no one could ever cut. He had told his Mrs once that he would never end up dying in old age in this town - he'd be in Dubai or some big *koti* back home but the truth was that he would. The only reality that he had to manage with *Allah mia* was the date of his departure.

Chapter Eleven

'Throughout the centuries there were men who took first steps, down new roads, armed with nothing but their own vision'

Ayn Rand

He surveyed the damage with a wry smile. Events had worked out better than expected with only the unfortunate death of some young white unemployed woman troubling him. He knew that in this war they would be white fatalities, he had come to look at it as an occupational hazard. Many of these poor white women were now the chattel of black and brown men and in these circumstances he was merely liberating them from this situation. She would have had further children with the Tamil man she was with. With her black friends & mixed race future partner she would have gone on to have brought further shame on her family & race.

The aftermath of these events were getting increasingly hard to handle & the old ways of 'fixing' the arrangements getting harder & harder.

The reason was twofold. One the layers of checks and commissioners that were building up - the odd uppity dark face probing away with their leftwing counterparts. The second reason was old age. Many of them were like him silver haired assassins past pensionable age but still keen to serve. The abduction of a Khan or a West Indian still mattered. Though he still hankered for a quiet life he did not want to descend into a Colonel Blimp figure in an armchair shouting impotently at the TV. But the new cadres coming up were not inspiring confidence. Many of them had got sloppy & allowed campaigners to focus on the slip ups identified. It was left to him and the other older ones to continue to carry the baton. What the future held was less certain but he knew the movement would continue like the ancient pathways still dotted around his beloved County.

Shiraz was keeping tracks on the night time economy. It was a phrase that he had heard at some consultative meeting and it had stuck in his head. No one really wanted to talk about the whores and their pimps, the junkies and their nutcase dealers so they would use this term. Sarge has called it an euphemism but Shiraz thought it was lazy and too polite. There were blokes in pubs blatantly dealing and local talent selling their pussies right in the faces of the local community. He knew some were on the case but they thought he was

(a) a traitor or (b) too stupid to grasp the reality of the situation. Now he would be the first to admit that he only ever read the News of the World and the sports page of the Jang but he had now gone on two in-service training programmes so he was on form and flying. He'd even borrowed a book on the Criminal Justice system that his eldest sister had been using as a doorstop. He was definitely going places.

This case though would not leave him alone. Visiting primary schools & warning six year olds over using knives & weapons did not occupy his mind. Frankly it was a waste of time as many of them came from families where the brothers had been tooled up as soon as they had hit double figures. No amount of 'preventative' work would be able to tackle that and the cops were the wrong people to be doing this. No, her face lingered in his mind & her *chehra would* be the last thing he saw at night & the first thing he would see in the morning. It bugged him & he could not work out why.

Some of Shiraz's fellow PCSO's were jokes - some of them were a joke and he wondered about the quality control. He stared across the room at the others who were sitting in on the Seminar. A selection of white, brown & black faces who were the community faces of the force. He stared at the guy immediately in front of him. Abdul was a fool, one of the biggest in a town that was not lacking in that department. There was good, sincere & honest folks in his manor but the overwhelming sense was of people engaged in stupidity & selfishness on a monumental scale. The trouble with Abs was that he was entirely status driven. But his ambition was not matched by his intelligence & the prick was always screwing up and making him &

other Asian & Caribbean officers look bad. Abdul would interfere in investigations and turn up at a Kashmiri household giving it the big man routine when there were already seniors there. Invariably they would laugh at him and he would end up making *chai* while the family put their feet up. He was about as useful as a pork chop in a Halal butchers in most instances and the funniest thing is that he never clocked on. Abdul continued to plough his career furrow down a steep hill and provided daily laughs for all down the station with a complete lack of self awareness. The brother was a joke.

Her face lingered in Asif's memories, she permeated his boxers, his socks and the inside of his *shalwar kameez.* Her imprint was deep inside his heart & he craved for her like Kas's crew craved their crack. The mad late night drives were a waste of petrol but he wanted to revisit the places they had screwed. The car park by the mausoleum by the golden ball was one place where their illicit couplings had been realised. Asif loved his wife but apart from bearing him children she only loved his passport. He had known the score from day one on account of him listening in to his parents calls back home. It was a marriage of convenience even though on a reality basis it was hassle, but once these issues were addressed both of them were pretty much free to do what wanted. For her it meant once she'd passed her driving lessons and acquired a Nissan Micra, spending time with her family in Coventry and her girlfriends in the town with kids in tow or with him if she went on any foreign missions. There was a roadmap to their relationship that they both adhered to regardless of the weather and prevailing winds. But now without Mandy he was now doing u-turns in a cul-de-sac going nowhere.

1913

Anna loved the days when spring finally arrived in the town. She could stay out longer on the days that the light stayed on, and her and her little collection of children in most need of correction could enjoy their adventures. They would follow the course of the Wye through crest beds and the meadows around Loudwater through the grotty town where all manner of debris was deposited on Sands and Dashwood's lands, where they would be chased by game keepers and assorted grounds men. They would go stickleback fishing and wade through the water searching for coins. One warm April Johnnie McManus, a relatively junior member of their gang found a bag of coins in a small ornate sack. After much squabbling and deliberation it was decided that Johnnie be allowed to keep the stash on account of his old man only having one leg and not being able to work and all.

This time the discovery was rather more unusual and disturbing. They had been down Oxford Road by the intersection with Bridge St when they had found the item. The Cornish twins Meg and Moe had been bombing underneath the bridges that ran from the main road to the outside of the terraced houses that lined the path. It had been a dry few weeks so the river level was low and despite the constant smell of Newlands around them and the fetid stagnant water they would dare themselves to run down through the arches and wade through to the other side. This time however the twins had been down there for several minutes, and Anna who always felt a sense of responsibility to her younger charges glanced anxiously downwards wondering if the water had claimed them. She heard them utter an almighty scream accompanied by loud shrieking as they emerged shaking and shivering

"It's a man - there's a man down there!" exclaimed Moe the slightly taller one with the big ears. Meg came up behind her dripping wet "But it's horrible he's got noooo" she coughed and stuttered as she struggled to get the words out.

"What hasn't he got?" demanded Annie in disbelief

In unison they both chanted "He's got no arms and legs!" Anna and her gang were in shock - they had discovered a limbless corpse on Oxford Road. All manner of murderous motivations filled her mind but she knew that she had to act as the twins and the rest of the motley crew could be in serious trouble. She got them to follow her up one of the alleys to a stretch of ground away from prying eyes and listening ears and convened a meeting. All of the gang realised that this was a serious situation as these meetings were unusually rare. Normally they would only be organised if they were at war with another crew. But ever since the Downley boys had received a public thrashing from one of the Constables that threat had subsided. Indeed PC Snelling had left his mark not only on the red crusty buttocks of the unfortunate boy but with the rest of the local un-correctables in the town.

"I have a plan"

Anna said with her arms folded behind her back after she had paced up and down whilst her acolytes waited for her deliberations. 'I don't know what's going on and what kind of evilness has done this but we got to tell the Bobbies Anna proclaimed looking at her crew for signs of reaction

"I'm not going to the Newlands cop house again not after what they did to my brother" said Maggot whose family had a number of dealings to do with the police on account of them being involved in petty thieving and such like

"I've not made my mind up who it will be yet though. We may need to write a note and deliver this to them."

They looked at each other wondering who would be nominated for this fearsome task and how this diminutive flame haired eleven year old girl exercised power over them. Since her 10th birthday she had seen off all the male competitors by fighting them on the land behind Desborough School. Her toothy grin was testimony to her tenacity and bravery.

Shadow of Eden

The road was wide. Sheep could be driven through without delay. The old ancient way connected the small town and its market to the outlying villages. This was the main artery which people and livestock would come through on many days of the week. There were other paths much smaller up and down the sides of the valley between Downley, West Wycombe and the town. You could disappear up these hollow ways away from the fields and pastures only to arrive up at the Common and during the day the sun would stream through the trees overhead. If you were caught at dusk you could be in trouble as gangs of robbers would await you if you were unlucky or you would slip down a ditch in the darkness. These paths criss-crossed the town hidden only by the woods and if you used them you could navigate the villages surrounding the town in an afternoon. Of course if it rained you were at the mercy of the elements and the paths and roads would be awash with storm water. One road in particular was particularly prone to flooding, so much so that it was named Watery Lane. The river and the streams that run through the town would overflow and the brown silty water would pour through the streets. Even a horse and carriage would find it heavy going and you would just have to wait till it subsided and normality returned to the world in the valley.

Years back it was said that there was a hospital for lepers and the diseased just off this road and it was then called St Margaret's Lane. It was named St. Giles after the patron saint of lepers and offered to alleviate all those that suffered. They were subsequently buried in the grounds that merged with the meadows and streams that were in the valley. The chalky waters were supposed to bring health and the many holy wells in the area were particular sources of this for the healers and the holy men. But the hospital fell into disrepair and the lepers were sent up to the north of the county. The grounds became a playground for local children and later a school was built closer to the road and children from both sides of the valley would come to the first school. There was a new name for the road – Desborough Road which was derived from the old name for the area and the old fort on the hill that overlooked this part of the town. The road was initially widened for the deliveries by horse drawn vehicles to the early furniture factories, and the many pubs that opened up for their workers and later for the first automobiles that came through. It wasn't long before a bus route ran through the length of the road connecting the hamlet of Sands and the newly formed communities in the fields of the castle, which had cut a path through the old mound that existed before the town itself.

The new shopping centre cast a shadow on the road. Not only did it ensure that most of the river was now concealed, but removed any sense that the town was in a valley. Those inhabitants who had the money scurried around from shop to shop making needless purchases and sipping their five pound coffees whilst the town's black and brown youth looked on with their low waged white brethren. The local taxi drivers denied sufficient pickings gorged themselves on cheap chicken and glimpses of flesh whilst bearded elders with bags of household goods rushed home to catch *zohr* prayers. A crowd of council *wallay* and their brown consorts milled through the crowds with the arrogance born of knowing that no one would ever challenge their judgement especially now that they had delivered the shiny shopping precinct. It did not matter that it had been built on slum lands and the sites of old furniture factories. The only references to the past were the quaint names of the windy alleys that had been created. Yes there had been fields here once and mills and ancient routes that linked the town to key strategic settlements in the Chilterns but these did not matter to Jessica sitting on the wall to the side of the bus station. Jessica was more concerned about her next fix and the undue attentions of Bash & Mangy.

Chapter Twelve

'Although the road is never ending take a step and keep walking, do not look fearfully into the distance. On this path let the heart be your guide for the body is hesitant and full of fear.'

Rumi

1913

The Wycombe police raised their batons and charged again at the crowd outside the factory gates. The furniture worker's protests were now into their second week and the pressure was on. Despite police reinforcements being called from London and several police and protesters being treated for injuries there seemed no signs of this crisis abating. Talks with the owners and leaders of the workers federation had broken down and even the calls for an end by the mayor and aldermen of the town had fallen on deaf ears.

There had been mysterious attacks on some of the organisers of the protests and a man's torso had been found in the Wye. The final straw was the unveiling of a large cloth banner proclaiming support for the strikers at a Wycombe Wanderers home match at Loakes Park.

She had the feeling that something was wrong when the Aldermen and the police turned up at their little terrace on Baker St. Anna had been outside the factory in the morning when the pickets were in force maintaining a steady presence. There were placards protesting about conditions in the furniture industry and the need for better pay. There were also banners from the Workers Federation and the new unions that were being setup around the country. What was happening in High Wycombe was big news not only for the town but for the country in the battle between labour and private capital. Anna went back in the evening to Desborough Road where crowds began to develop and she took a gang with her. Some of these kids had little idea what was going on but were feeling the stress and pain at home. Then there were the battle ready ones like her and Big Jake who had started to read the papers, make the links and could see the gross inequality that was being laid out in front of them. The success of the furniture industry town had come at much cost and it was their families at the bottom who were paying for it.

She listened to the speeches and the fine words from the great and good and also the not so good. Her father had warned her about the latter group:

"They will look like us and even talk like us but they are not part of our struggle - in many ways they are the enemy dressed up in workers clothing."

She would listen intently; her young mind soaking this up like a fancy sponge that would be on display in the local Haberdashery shop with a label saying it would soak up a gallon of water.

"Some of our leaders have done deals; they've sold us up the river. Mind you there'll be trouble: we're not going to take this lying down I swear."

He looked at Anna with his clear blue eyes and told her to go to bed and as she made space on the mattress that she shared with her brothers and sisters she remembered his words.

Her father was on the small stage that had been erected and was about to speak. Out of the corner of her eye she saw police officers assemble and members of the Anti Violence Brigade surround the stage. There was trouble brewing and the last few nights there had been fights and scuffles. She'd heard that PC Snelling and the other bobbies had asked for reinforcements from London but did not know if this was a scare tactic. Anna's Dad was speaking now and in front of her had become transferred into Kevin Shaw a vanguard figure in the struggles locally. He had a reputation for being a fiery figure who told it as it was, and today was no exception. He laid into the factory owners, the Aldermen and Councillors, the police and the scabs. Anna's Dad was in full flow when the heckling started and something was thrown towards him. Before then she'd noticed the clicking of fingers and hand actions and she figured something was up. There was a scuffle at the front and she had to tip toe to see what was happening. She saw the police and the AVB confront each other and the crowds went crazy. She must have been hit by something as she remembered Big Jake picking her up and then the rest of the night was a mystery.

The policeman walked into the room followed by the Alderman. She knew what he was going to say as it could only be the most severe news that she could imagine.

"Your Daddy's dead Anna; he had an accident. I think he fell off the stage at the protest and cracked his head and we lost him. He was a good fella your old man"

She got up slowly and went over to her Dads old coat and hugged it with tears streaming down her face.

The Alderman gestured to the policeman and they left the room.

"Speak to the Mother about the funeral arrangements and you make sure that the family gets some money to tide them over. We don't want another destitute family in Newlands"

The officer nodded and he walked out into Desborough Road.

"Oh by the way - make sure you cover up those marks on his face and his neck. We don't want to upset the poor dears do we?"

1981

'I still walk this same old lonely street

Still trying to find, find a reason

Policeman comes and smacks me in the teeth

I don't complain, it's not my function'

The Specials 'Do Nothing'

The rioting had spread to Desborough Road and targeted some of the white businesses. The police had not managed to contain it around St Mary's Street as planned. They had arrested several West Indian and Pakistani young men in skirmishes where they came under attack. Police reinforcements had been called from other parts of the County where things were relatively peaceful. However up and down the country rioting was widespread as young people attacked public property and police officers. In Wycombe despite the interventions of the local MP and the small mosque located in a house on Jubilee Road the rioting continued. The smell of smoke filled the air and people trampled on broken glass underfoot.

Mohinder was angry - not only had he been stopped by the police driving into Frogmoor but his bag of tools had been taken from him, as in the words of the officer who had detained him; 'there was a lot of thieving going on in town'. He was well behind the Black youth in the town - all the younger West Indian and Pakistani brothers and the odd sister who were taking the battle to the cops. Frankly in his opinion they deserved it and though he'd supported his cousin brother who had admonished his son for getting involved in the riots in Birmingham he was secretly proud of his nephew for standing up to the Babylon as the Rasta boys called them. He knew that his brother in arms Mohammed Hussain also felt the same way but on account of their older years they had to seen to be mature and sensible. He could feel that there was trouble brewing and though they had managed to deal with the local skinheads by uniting with other *kalay* so they were now 'under manners' he was less confident about taking on the local fuzz. The cops were seriously tooled up now and since Brixton and Liverpool and dem boys were kicking off they were now ready with their riot shields and new extended batons. He had felt a baton on the side of his head a few years back when he joined with other Sikhs and other Asians in the town to protest about Sikh men having to wear helmets. In particular the banner that the local trade union delegation had brought down was especially memorable - it had read 'An injury to ONE is an injury to ALL' but the funny thing is that none of those union fuckers got wacked in the head by cops as the protest got a bit wild. He was lucky that his *pagri* had caught the blow otherwise he could have been killed like that Blair Peach *larka.*

Hussain *Bhai* was getting nervous. It was hard enough making sure his kids stayed in but when older members of the community had given him the responsibility to keep an eye on their sons during the rioting it was almost impossible. He had never been a babysitter or changed a nappy in his life. But now he was being asked to look after grown boys.

"*Bhai* these *munday* respect you - you can speak to them in English and tell them to behave *yaara*"

As ever it was difficult to say no but it was a hard job as at least one boy in each of the roads had access to a *gaddi* so they would all pile in. Walking on foot in groups had been clamped down on so the car was the only way. He knew that it was going to turn nasty and that the Black boys in town especially the West Indians would not let things go as there were certain police officers who were straight up racist *bhenchods* that caused grief to all coloureds in the town.

They'd sealed off St Mary's Street - the whole area under the flyover and the pubs close by were effectively a no go area. But he needed to get a prescription in town and decided to walk in so he could assess the damage himself. As he got closer to Bridge Street he could see a number of shops boarded up and glass everywhere and there was a big crowd in the car park close by. He could hear voices of local youth recounting what police had been doing over the years and the beats that some of them had got in the last few days. Few of them wanted to march to the police station on Queen Elizabeth Street to protest and once this seemed to get the vote the crowd started to move towards Newlands Tesco's. He followed them maintaining a little distance and to check if any of his nephews or cousins were involved. Hussain spotted Bilal's boy Taufiq with his permed hair and gold chain, a look a lot of the Asian boys now favoured. He didn't call him but just watched as he laughed and joked with the rest of them. This motley collection of black and brown rude boys would pose a serious challenge to the local *marvay* but he was worried about the police being ready for them. The first few nights had caught the cops by surprise but there were rumours that the police had increased their numbers.

He spotted a group of younger kids that were with their brothers –
there was young Danish Raja whose Mum called him Danny after
some long forgotten pop star and a few others who must have been
five or six years old. He went over to their brothers to have a word

"Oi *larkay* take these little ones home they shouldn't be here. Their
Mums will be worried to death"

They didn't bother arguing with him but that little fucker Danny Raja
stuck his tongue out at him as he was leaving and he knew that boy
would be a handful when he grew up.

Hussain was glad he sent them home as a line of coppers appeared to
stop the lads getting to the town centre. He knew their game now,
they were going to try to force the crowd back to Bridge Street and
the Desborough Road area. The police thinking would be that if they
started to kick off then they wanted to keep them in our own areas
so they would end up trashing their own shops rather than the town
centre. He heard from friends in Leicester and Bradford that the cops
were using this tactic. Businesses were closing up early or even
closing completely as staff were increasingly getting too frightened
to come into work and companies were getting nervous about losing
trade. The only people who were making money during this time
were the insurance *wallay*, the fitters who were boarding up shops
left right and centre and all the cops on double time. As the youth
held their line further vans of police reinforcements appeared with
riot shields being seen through the windows. Police were tooled up
and looking for a fight and he knew that he would have to leave
pretty soon otherwise he too would get caught get up in the action.

He turned to move but his way was blocked by another line of officers and they were penned in and surrounded. Youths started to grab anything that could be used as a weapon and all of a sudden he was caught up in a war that was unfolding on the roads around him. Hussain saw a young Pakistani boy with a metal pole in his hand be surrounded by a mass of blue and others taking baton blows. He ducked down as bricks were thrown towards a phalanx of shields that had come together just by the roundabout with Oxford Road but he felt a blow to his head and was knocked to the ground and as he touched his head he could feel a steady flow of blood. As he tried to get to his feet he saw young Danny Raja come towards him:

"Un-kal?"

He had tears streaming down his face and Hussain grabbed him and picked him up in his arms and ran to the line of Officers who on seeing him with a child parted to make way for him. Hussain acknowledged this act and nodded his head.

"Get that kid out and get that cut seen to fella"

The copper had said and as he rushed past him he remembered thinking that maybe not all these coppers were bastards but when he turned and looked back he saw the lads getting such a vicious beating he quickly changed his mind.

"Un-kal look *khoon khoon*"

Danny had blood on him from the cut that Hussain had sustained and was now on the boys top so he took out a *rumaal* from his back pocket and put it over the wound.

"*Chul putar* let's get you go home – your Mum's going to kill me!"

He knew that the abuse that he would get from Danny's Mum would be nothing compared to the punishment the police were handing out behind him. She would calm down and be thankful that Hussain had brought him home and there would be roti and some nice munch. But these boys would be spending the night either in a cell or in intensive care and those would be the lucky ones. He was sure that they would kill a black lad in the town tonight and hoped that Allah, God or Jah would protect them in these merciless times.

Chapter Thirteen

'Call the worker to leave his toil,

Call the clerk from the office stool;

Let the farmer forsake the soil,

And the youth troop forth from the school,

Come and march, all ye men of the nation!

All whose hearts are not frosted with fear,

We are waging a war of salvation,

And the hour of decision is here!

Come all Young Britain, and march with the

Blackshirt Battalions!

England awake!

Forward to the future, for that shall be ours!'

British Union of Fascists marching song

He was getting restless. He had not received the message from his superiors and had too much time on his hands. As he got older and hopefully wiser, with the advancing years key incidents and occasions came back to him starkly and vividly. His childhood, his adolescent years and his previous name and the life associated with it. He had not always been the Assassin.

One of his most vivid memories was meeting the infamous Mitford sisters as a four year old and thinking how beautiful Diana one of the more prominent sisters was. This was just at the end of the 30's before the British Union of Fascists had been banned after the Second World War had started. The Mitford family had a summer residence in High Wycombe near Bassetbury Manor. His father who he later found out had been one of the 'Bright Young Things' of the 20's, a group of up and coming rising stars of High Society, had taken him to see the Mitfords at the age of four. As he later found out, he, and these individuals were destined for the highest offices of the land and a life of wealth, debauchery and racial supremacy.

He remembered being driven up to Handy Cross which in those days was still a small village area with only a few settlements around it. Papa then turned into a farm which he later identified was Winchbottom Farm and where he was introduced to local Blackshirt leaders who through the kind permission of local landowners had set up a camp to recruit and train local people and those from further afield. These pure white Aryan recruits with their ruddy complexions were to be Britain's master race. But he remembered looking at this weedy collection of middle and upper class fellows and feeling slightly ashamed. Maybe that was why during the war some of the women folk went with Negro GI's in the town. Many of them were fine specimens of men and even he as an eugenic white supremacist could see this. However a few people stood out from this group, and the gracious faces of the Mitford girls particularly so. He heard that during the war many of these people were interned by the Government and one of the highlights of his younger years was receiving a letter from Diana Mitford whilst she was in prison thanking him for his concern but declining his offer to be her pen pal.

In many ways that early visit to Winchbottom was the turning point that got him started on this particular road of justice and his noble cause. Whether his Dad realised this he was not sure as the old fellow subsequently disappeared and ended up as a washed up alcoholic in an obscure colonial outpost. From the age of eight he had started to keep a scrapbook of the activities of the fascist groups in England and on his eighteenth birthday in 1953 he joined the nascent Union party with Oswald Mosley who had now taken up with Diana. He was not sure what his mother had meant when she had mentioned this but from the tone of her voice it was not the 'done thing' at the time.

Why were these memories coming back to him so vividly? In the recent weeks he had been grappling with the fact that he was aging and however skilled and experienced he was sooner or later this would catch up with him. His left hand had occasionally begun to shake and he was experiencing low energy levels. However much he wanted to carry on what he and the others could not afford was a slip up or a mistake that could jeopardize their mission. He had informed Raven HQ through the required back channels of his intention to retire. They would allow him to slip away out of sight and even induce dementia and encourage memory loss. He also knew that he too could be removed if necessary if it was felt that he knew too much. There would be no gold watch situation or any grand send off - discretion was always maintained. But he knew that one way or another he would be looked after.

He was still awaiting a set of final instructions - whether to stand down or perhaps if he was lucky a final mission as a goodbye present. There was still some unresolved business with this Pakistani taxi driver and self hating journalist sniffing around as well as a local ethnic Police and Community Support Officer who was trying to make a name for himself. They needed to be dealt with or at least given a few false leads to throw them off the trail.

His mind wandered to the sixties when he first became a GP and adopted the moniker as the Assassin and how he stood proudly in the audience when Enoch Powell had come to town. That master orator and fondly remembered fellow fascist had found much support for his views in Wycombe and in South Bucks. Whilst he had no truck with the boot boys in the London docks and the shaven headed thugs that would be a common sight on the streets of High Wycombe they did serve a purpose. They gave cover for more of the insidiously brutal missions that he and his associates would carry out.

There was the old Caribbean couple that he'd prescribed sleeping tablets to as work was taking place in their area as the new motorway came to town. By altering the dosage and masking his tracks he was able to further reduce the population in the town. His greatest hatred was reserved for the Asians and the Pakistanis and Kashmiris that had come over because of a dam being built that was going to flood their villages. This population had brought over the old subcontinent habit of breeding like rabbits and within a few years had populated key parts of the town in big numbers. The ironic aspect that one of the main settlements was close to an ancient leprosy hospital that had existed on the old road. Hundreds of years later the disease that had afflicted many in times gone by was still there in his eyes and was manifested in these half human animals who dared to infect his beloved home. The first time he had terminated a child it had been difficult. When this method of population control had been explained to him it made absolute sense. But carrying out for the first time had troubled him and he had not been prepared for the anguish that followed. What probably made it worse was the nonchalant attitude of the Punjabi father who was most likely just going to go back home, blame his wife and then impregnate her again!

The approach had been made to him after the 1962 Immigration Act as large numbers of Asians and West Indians were joining their brethren in the so called Motherland. Whilst fascists views were officially sidelined as the spectre of the War still hung over the country there were good people in positions of power who were extremely distressed by the levels of coloured immigrants entering the country. A small group - Raven's People were prepared to do something about it and it was they who sought him out. He remembered the day when he received a verbal request by a minor member of the local gentry for a meeting. He was given instructions to meet at a particular bar in the local town where he met a gentleman who escorted him to a car in which he was subsequently blindfolded. After what seemed to be a thirty minute journey he was escorted out of the car still wearing the blindfold and led to a dark room where three people proceeded to ask him questions. He answered truthfully and was accepted and inducted into this organisation. The next four decades or so just seemed to whizz by with mission after mission until he found himself in 2007. He knew that there might be a final grand flourish, a final applet to decades of missions across the towns of the County. There was no major settlement where he had not left his mark, no roads that he had not travelled down but the question was whether he would be allowed a final curtain call to end his time on this Buckinghamshire stage. He opened his briefcase and took out a phone. From his wallet he took out this month's sim card and placed it in the phone. He switched it on and read the message.

Chapter Fourteen

'The one duty we owe to history is to rewrite it'

Oscar Wilde

Something was not quite right. Stacey could feel it. The town had returned back to normal within a few weeks. That was straight forward in itself - people had lives to lead and politicians had their lies to conceal. It was that months after Mandy's murder there were too many questions still unanswered. Why kill a sex worker as a warning? To leave the body in a skip was just perhaps too obvious. Crucially however there was no inkling about who it was that had done this. All the usual suspects were just too predictable. Of course mainstream media wanted to racialise it - there was talk of Yardies and Eastern European crews as well as some Punjabi/Kashmiri nexus of activity. Stacey was getting wise to this scaremongering and scatter gun approach. Her father in a rare moment of honesty and lucidity (he was stoned at his brother's house) had shared with her his thoughts about organised gangs in Buckinghamshire:

"It's us white bastards! Well I mean white but there's this smattering of European types in the mix as well - your Frenchies and some of those Mediterranean sorts"

He proceeded to tell her about the fascist gangs that used to exist around London and the Home Counties in the 30's. How the Country wasn't united against the Third Reich and how they all went underground during the war only to emerge again in the 50's and 60's as respectable establishment racists.

She'd gone away and done some research about the established families in the town and the links to both local government and local industry. It appeared that some of these key individuals were not only busy making well crafted chairs but were also creating the furniture for the seating arrangements of power in High Wycombe. They were not just making chairs they were becoming Chairmen themselves. All manner of low and underhand behaviour could follow these developments. Recent terror events had made her push this out of her mind but she was now returning to these thoughts and trying to link the dots together. She would keep digging and follow her instincts - there was an invisible set of hands at work here and she would not rest till she uncovered them.

The case would still not leave Shiraz and he could not leave the case alone. He'd had a disciplinary over his involvement with the Mandeep investigation and where it was cited that he was behaving unprofessionally and letting his feelings on the case cloud his judgment. But he knew something was wrong - there were too many unanswered questions and aspects of the investigation just too hastily constructed. It was almost as if they had decided the outcome before the investigation had even begun. The Seniors seem to be exceptionally touchy about anything to do with the death. CID were even more closed and secretive than normal - anyone would think that this was terror related or a matter of national security. It had not been issued with a command status and none of the great and good had descended on the town so apart from the normal pronouncements there was little to report.

But Shiraz had a nagging feeling that the town was being duped and he and other Asians and the blacks were being played. It wasn't the way that the town returned to normality so quickly or the community leaders falling over themselves to make their empty statements. He was new to this policing game but alarm bells were ringing about how quickly the case was closed and the internal memo that went out within hours confirmed his suspicion:

'Please be aware that this case has been closed now. All lines of inquiry have been exhausted and unless any new unequivocal evidence emerges no further investigation will be taking place.'

He stared at the touch screen of his phone and went to a couple of contacts in the directory. He needed to keep an eye of things and there were a couple of people he would need to keep an eye on to do this. Even though Shiraz was wary of Asif he knew that his fellow Pakistani would not let this lie. The people from his village back home and the *biradari* here were known for holding grudges and being relentless. As someone who could have been the last person to see Mandy alive he would perhaps hold the key to who killed her and why.

He would need to keep tabs on Stacey not because he found the outlines of her shoulder blades alluring but because Shiraz recognised her ability to dig and ask questions. Apparently she was not satisfied with the received version of events even though she'd been responsible for regurgitating key parts of it when she broke the story. He'd found out from a cute Indian *kuree* in the media unit that she was still pestering the police with Freedom of Information (FOI) requests. He'd done the one day media training and knew that only someone who had some dirt on the cops or the investigation would persist with this line of enquiry.

But most importantly what Stacey had was something that both he and Asif were severely lacking in - her whiteness. It had taken only a few months in his employment as a Police and Community Support Officer for him to work out what that meant. Her whiteness meant that she was part of the club, that she understood the rules and how to chat and be at ease in both formal and informal settings. However much he and his fellow darkies tried to integrate they would always be caught out. Some of the Caribbean lads could play along with the banter and the chit chat but when it got to a certain level they would be left in the slow lane whilst these *goray* would be putting their foot down. Just cos Pakistanis has the latest wheels didn't mean they were going anywhere - most of them would be stuck in the hard shoulder watching life pass them by. That's what whiteness really meant. He knew instinctively at Grammar school that even the dumb white fuckers who only had a handful of GCSEs would be alright, would be sorted because as well as having rich Mummies and Daddies they were well connected. Only a very few Pakistanis operated like this as well as some the Indian families that he knew. There were other things at play; big and powerful lobbies and people he was only just beginning to understand. The rich and the mighty in the town were hiding something and he would really have to be break his back to get to the bottom of this particular puzzle.

Asif was determined to find Mandy's killers. But he wasn't going to bang some heads he was going to speak to a few youth workers and some of the local lads to set up a campaign. There were even a few lawyer type sisters who were well connected who could help. He'd been thinking about his options and what he could physically do. In the old days he would have thought nothing of getting some of the boys together but he was still very much a suspect and on the radar of the cops. Asif knew that he needed to play this clever and yea the whole legal campaign thing could cost him money, time and probably his hair - but he had no choice and owed it to her big time.

He'd go and see a few people he knew would be down with what he wanted to do and would not be phased to take on the powers that be. There seemed to be stuff happening behind the scenes, information that he was not party to. He couldn't put his finger on it but it probably involved the police and maybe some of the well known network of brown and black informants in the town. These pricks walked around with impunity even when they were still shotting and engaged in some serious criminal activity operating as if they were untouchable. Then there were those who pretended to be community mediators who were the first to appear on the scene if there was any trouble but who were on the payroll of the local police and brazenly paraded this as almost a badge of honour.

Out of all this mess he would find a way to the truth, even if he had to drive down every road in the town or the county. He would leave no stone unturned - Mandy had been found in a skip on West Richardson Street and Asif was prepared to dig through any files or paperwork and attend any amount of bogus meetings to find out who had killed her. She'd lived as the kids said nowadays 'on road' and maybe it was these roads that killed her. They were full of perverted Pakistanis and raging Poles, full of white men with Mummy and power issues - too many pricks with a point to prove against womenkind and with an axe to grind.

Stacey did not see the Zafira coming down the road as she went to the bank. She did not see it mount the kerb and hit a bollard. Nor did she feel it as it slammed her body against the shop front spraying glass everywhere.

Asif took a deep breath and let the spliff drop down through his fingers to the mat below. Thoughts raced through his mind as he gradually picked up speed as he focused on his latest mission. He stared down at the photo of Mandeep in the newspaper on the passenger seat. He did not see Anjum at the cash point using fake cards to get out some dosh and he did not see the white woman as he ploughed into her.

Shiraz ran to the scene and immediately saw that the woman had been almost sliced in half by the car. He knew he only had seconds to act if the driver and any passengers were to be saved. He managed to open the door and saw Asif semi-conscious at the wheel. He was not wearing a belt but even then it was hard to move him. Shiraz knew that the engine would go at any moment and he tried to get close to the driver. He felt a hand grip him tight on his arm and turned back to see Asif staring at him.

Police report:

"The vehicle exploded on the corner of West Richardson St and Desborough Avenue at approximately 10.30am yesterday morning. Three people were killed during this accident. A woman bystander local journalist Stacey Shaw, the driver of the vehicle Asif Hussain and PCSO Shiraz Ali who bravely attempted to save the driver and was caught up when the vehicle exploded. Foul play is not suspected but checks are being carried out on the vehicle."

Press Conference Statement:

"This is a tragic & unfortunate accident. It is always a very sad day for us when we lose any local citizens but to lose three is quite difficult to understand. Contrary to local gossip and rumor the nature of the incident was purely accidental and we have no reason to believe that the brakes in the vehicle had been tampered with or that the driver Mister Hussain who hit the pedestrian had been killed on purpose. Claims that bruising had been found on the Community Support Officer's arms are completely unconnected with the incident and we do not welcome any conjecture on this matter. Such loss of life is regrettable and our condolences go out to all the families in particular those of PCSO Ali who had been in post less than 6 months."

MP statement

'My sympathies go out to the families involved in this horrific incident. I think we need to ensure that we do not make any premature statements at this stage and allow the police and the relevant authorities to complete their investigations. I will be visiting the scene in the next few days and speaking to local community leaders who are on the ground. The Desborough Road area of High Wycombe gets a terrible press at the best of times but we are determined to ensure that this part of town retains its unique character and historical importance. I ask all the communities to stay calm and collected during this time'

Independent Advisory Group/Our Wycombe statement

'We stand with all the communities at this sad time and have full confidence in the police and the authorities to investigate this incident. We will be offering prayers for Shiraz and Asif and have passed on condolences to the family of Stacy Shaw. It is important that we stand together as one town and are united in our grief and sadness at this time. We reject any line of questioning that does not correspond to the given police narrative and ask all our young people in particular to stay calm and not point a finger at anyone. We assure you all that the Independent Advisory Group will continue to meet with our police friends to look at this matter and Our Wycombe will remain a united voice on this issue.'

EPILOGUE

She got off at the bus station and walked towards the hill. She saw people spilling out of Second Hand City who had been busy selling their furniture and worldly belongings. The gentlemen inside were rubbing their hands and patting themselves on the back. Behind the pub the shopping centre remained closed with only the charred paintwork and broken windows giving any clue to what had happened.

It was getting cold as she went passed the church and she saw two police officers doing a vehicle check as a pale complexioned young woman dashed around the corner to avoid them. She heard the driver swearing under his breath in Punjabi and chuckled to herself. The *Marvay* always got you in the end and these little boys never realised it till it was too late. It started to rain and she picked up an umbrella from a haberdashery store, even though she had the wrong coins the kind old women took pity on her and gave her one in exchange for a two pound coin. The wind blew in gusts and thick black smoke seemed to be all round her as man cycled past. All of a sudden the road got narrower and narrower until it was only wide enough for the cart and horses which were passing. She saw the fires burning from the fort on the hill and she walked towards the light as trees and bushes surrounded her on both sides. She came to the front of the Castle and looked up at the copse of trees that had started to grow around it. She sat by the fire and waited.

Glossary

Bhai jhaan	Older brother
Angrez	English
Nnukray	Fussiness
Ladoos	Asian sweets
Hakeem	Doctor
Bheta	Son
Abbo	Father
Pindi	Shortened version of the word Rawalpindi, a city in Pakistan
Chowkidaar	Caretaker/Security guard
Gobi	Cauliflower (also a nickname for a local lad!)
Chacha	Paternal uncle
Yayrah	Friend
Mahvay	Police
Larkee	Girl
Paisa	Money
Kalmah	Islamic saying
Maal	Drugs

Aloo Gobi	Potatoes & cauliflower
Jummah	Friday
Goray	White people
Khaana	Dinner
Kutta	Dog
Kismet	Destiny
Jullander	Town in Punjab
Mungater	Newly arrived immigrant
Kusmay	Promise
Haldi	Turmeric
Ammi	Mother
Shaytaan	Devil
Chadees	Shorts/underwear
Chitta gora	White skinned
Gulabs	Roses
Tutta	Testicle
Shehar	Area/neighbourhood
'Zindagi ka yeh safar	'This life is a journey

Koi samjhe to nahin	That no one understands
Yehi rasta hai mera	This road is mine
Koi aata hi nahin'	And I am on my own'
Qayamat	Day of Judgment in Islam
Chumchay	Stooges
Shair	Poetry
Angreezi	English language
Munda korn hai?	Who is this boy?
Sardar	Sikh man
Pihari	Mountain dialect
Theek hai	Ok
Yaar	friend
Salee	Sister in law
Kuffar	Non-believer
Sharam	Shame
Zuhr	Midday prayer
Waallay	People
Goree	White girl

Avsoos	Mourning
Kurbistan	Cemetery
Kotee	Big house
Roti	Flatbread
Choosa	Baby chicken
Jaan	Darling
Theek ho	Are you ok?
Chehra	Face
Karlay	Blacks
Moochay	Mustaches
Munday	Men
Chul putaar	Go kid
Larka/Larkay	Boys/Boys
Bhainjoots	Sister fuckers
Khoon	Blood
Biradari	Male kin/family
Kuree	Girl

References

1. Royal Jews by Jonathan Romain 2013

2. Remapping High Wycombe: journeys beyond the western sector John Rogers 2005-2006

3. 'Home to Home': A history of Asians in High Wycombe A Chaudhri 1988

4. 'Report on excavations at Desborough Castle, High Wycombe' M Collard 1987

5. 'High Wycombe Past' J Rattue 2002

6. 'Wycombe is something else' A report into experiences of Black and Asian youth in Wycombe town centre 1989

7. Bucks Free Press & Guardian archives

Song lyrics

1. 'Signs' (Cleve Bright) Badmarsh & Shri Outcast Records 2001

2. 'Lebanese Blonde' (Hilton/Garza) Thievery Corporation 4AD 1998

3. 'Dirty Old Town' (Ewan McColl) The Pogues Stiff Records 1985

4.   'Khwaab' (N Chag) Niraj Chag Buzz-erk Records 2007

5.   'Wake up and Live' (B Marley) Bob Marley & the Wailers Island Records1979

6.   'Do Nothing' The Specials (L Golding) Two-Tone Records 1980

Acknowledgements

SWOP service

Arts4everyone

ABOUT THE AUTHOR

Saqib Deshmukh was born in South London in 1967. He has worked all over the country as a youth worker and he settled in High Veecombe/Wycombe in 1997. He has been writing since 1984 and published a collection of his poetry TIMEBOMB in 1992 and has been published in newspapers, magazines and anthologies as well as some dodgy publications that he would rather not talk about.

Additionally he also been a music promoter, a DJ, an Arts trainer/Tutor, and managed bands such as THE KALIPHZ, as well as setting up theatre companies AIR theatre (1984-1989) and AAJKAL Theatre (1989- 1993 & 1999-2001). He has set up a production company INDUS VALLEY FUNK PRODUCTIONS to do stupid creative things and regularly works as a writer in schools, community centres and for local aunties.

In the last six years he has been a campaigner around deaths in custody after the death of a Pakistani man literally on his doorstep and has worked with the family to set up the Justice4Paps campaign. He fears that this has now labeled him as a domestic extremist and that the police are 'after him'. The local police declined to comment on this accusation.

In his spare time he likes to eat and sleep.

Made in the USA
Charleston, SC
28 November 2014